Bacchanalia

A Pamplona Story

Published by Coolbrook Avenue Press

5435 Coolbrook Avenue, H3X 2L3

Montreal, QC, Canada

ISBN-10:1708890548

ISBN-13: 978-1708890544

Imprint: Independently published

Cover photo by Jim Hollander

Cover design by Michael Hemingway

For Kristina

Ernest Hemingway once wrote, "Pamplona is no place to bring your wife." But the devil of it is that he never said anything about whether one can possibly *find* a wife in Pamplona. He left that to his grandson, John Hemingway, whose new novel *Bacchanalia, A Pamplona Story* offers a modern-day look at the celebration that is known as the Fiesta of San Fermin in Pamplona. Like his grandfather's 1926 masterpiece, *The Sun Also Rises*, John Hemingway's *Bacchanalia* is an entertaining and captivating story of a cast of colorful expats and locals during this annual event that descends upon an otherwise ordinary city every July in the Navarre region of northeastern Spain.

But don't think this is an attempt at cloning or channeling the elder Hemingway's story or style, far from it. In fact, the protagonist, Frank Ardito, makes but passing reference to Papa, noting that "Frank himself was not a great fan of Ernest Hemingway. He had read him, of course, and as a writer he respected his talent but his taste in literature lay elsewhere." And while John also acknowledges that the Fiesta attracts legions of participants each year who are "aficionados of the author who absolutely had to do everything and be everywhere Hemingway had been," the characters in this novel aren't such folks. That's not to say that the female love interest, the beautiful and captivating Irina, doesn't have more than a little Brett Ashley in her. But I'll leave that to the reader to ponder.

The underlying premise of the story is that, in life, there are times and places where it's perfectly acceptable, if not mandatory, to suspend the day-to-day conventions, morals and responsibilities of mundane, everyday life and let one's hair down. Eat, drink and be merry, for tomorrow we die, and all that rot. We're all familiar with the "What happens in Vegas" slogan, as well as Mardi Gras in New Orleans, college Spring Break in Florida and Mexico, Carnival in Rio, Fantasy Fest in Key West, and all of the other examples of "get your sinning out of your system, then go back to your boring life." Jake Barnes, the protagonist in *The Sun Also Rises* summed it up pretty succinctly: "Everyone behaves badly. Give them the proper chance." That's the Fiesta, that's *Bacchanalia* in a nutshell. But what separates this Fiesta (and this novel) from the others is that it's set against the tragedy of the Spanish bullfight, the centuries-old, inexplicable and indefensible tradition of man against bull, where while the man might lose, the bull will never win.

Bacchanalia is centered around a colorful collection of friends who've been gathering in Pamplona for the Fiesta for some ten years. There's Frank, an Italian-American poet/house painter from Los Angeles; Hector, a Chicano, former semi-pro boxer (and bipolar) writer from San Diego; Clive, a former Royal Air Force pilot from the UK; Ian, a "Scottish hipster"; and Peter, a former Navy Seal. All of them assemble each year for the camaraderie, the food, drink and debauchery, and the running of the bulls each morning. For some, the Fiesta is cathartic. For Hector, Pamplona offers him the ability to discontinue his Lithium; running with the bulls at each morning's *encierro* gave him a high that produce "god-like sensations." For Peter, this same thrill is a novel form of therapy for the PTSD he brought home from his Navy

6

Seal deployment in Afghanistan. Sure, they were all grown men with presumably responsible lives back home, but each year's Fiesta offered them a chance for fellowship, healing and release.

On the topic of the fiesta, Hemingway (Ernest, I mean) also noted that if you *did* happen to bring your wife to Pamplona, "the odds are all in favor of her getting ill, hurt or wounded or at least jostled and wine squirted all over her, or of losing her; maybe all three. ... It's a man's fiesta and women at it make trouble, never intentionally of course, but they nearly always make or have trouble. ... Of course if she can talk Spanish so she knows she is being joked with and not insulted, if she can drink wine all day and all night and dance with any group of strangers who invite her, if she does not mind things being spilled on her, if she adores continual noise and music and loves fireworks, especially those that fall close to her or burn her clothes, if she thinks it is sound and logical to see how close you can come to being killed by bulls for fun and for free, if she doesn't catch cold when she is rained on and appreciates dust, likes disorder and irregular meals and never needs to sleep and still keeps clean and neat without running water; then bring her. You'll probably lose her to a better man than you."

Within the pages of *Bacchanalia,* the reader is asked to ponder that very question, which offers a tension that runs throughout the novel: will Frank lose Irina to a better man than he? One gets the sense that, as long as the nine-day bacchanalia is running its course, anything could happen, all bets are off. Just like at the Fiesta itself, you might have to wait until the ending.

I note that the elder Hemingway chose a quotation from Ecclesiastes as the epilogue for *The Sun Also Rises,* one with which many are familiar:

"One generation passeth away, and another generation cometh; but the earth abideth forever... The sun also ariseth, and the sun goeth down, and hasteth to the place where he arose... The wind goeth toward the south, and turneth about unto the north; it whirleth about continually, and the wind returneth again according to his circuits.... All the rivers run into the sea; yet the sea is not full; unto the place from whence the rivers come, thither they return again."

Nearly a century later, I'm reminded of another passage from Ecclesiastes, which could also describe Pamplona's Fiesta and the younger Hemingway's novel: "Then I commended mirth, because a man hath no better thing under the sun, than to eat, and to drink, and to be merry." For nine days every July, and within the pages of this entertaining read, that's the mantra for the characters populating the cafés, clubs, streets and pages of *Bacchanalia.* And, who knows, perhaps this Fiesta won't be just nine days of frivolity and merrymaking, perhaps something lasting will come of the story. Isn't it pretty to think so?

Bacchanalia

A Pamplona Story

Chapter 1

At exactly a minute before twelve noon Frank stood in what he imagined to be more or less the middle of the "mosh pit" of the *Ayuntamiento,* although it was hard to say with the irregular waves of people who were pushing him first to the left and then to the right, a few steps forward and then ten steps back. Above him there were giant inflatable beach balls bouncing off the arms of the crowd that propelled them from one side of the square to the other, while a sangria drenched woman to his left sat laughing and ecstatic on the shoulders of her boyfriend as others reached up to touch her. The roar of the voices of the many thousands crammed into an area that had become a riotous sea of color and emotion impatiently awaited the beginning of the *Fiesta.*

It was the party to beat all parties, the bacchanalia, which lasted nine days and nine nights, and Frank was there again in the place that he loved perhaps more than any other, in the town that had first seduced him and then had saved him from himself.

"*Pamplonesas!*" shouted the mayor from the balcony of the City Hall. "*Pamploneses! Viva San Fermín, Gora San Fermín!*"

The *fiesta* had begun. The rocket was lit and the crowd exploded.

Chapter 2

Frank was checking his Instagram feed when he looked at his watch and remembered that it was time to meet the Russian psychiatrist. The appointment was at half past five but he knew that with the crowds on the first day of the *fiesta* it would take forever to get there.

"Do you want to come?" Frank asked his friend, who was lying on the sofa but who also felt that it was time to get up and rejoin the party.

"Why not?" he answered.

The two of them had sublet the apartment for the duration of the *fiesta*. They both lived in California. Frank was from L.A. and Hector was from San Diego, but they'd met in Spain while running with the bulls. They had known each other for more than a decade and when they weren't in Pamplona they would get together as often as they could for drinks, surfing or the occasional pro boxing match.

"Now who is this guy?" asked Hector, as he put on his running shoes.

"Like I said, he's a Russian, he's a shrink and he wants to meet me."

"He's a shrink and he wants to meet you, that's interesting. You got some problems that maybe I should know about, Frank?"

"Nah, don't be an idiot, the guy's into poetry."

"Ah, that stuff you write, I get it."

"Yeah, that stuff I write, we're going to Café Iruña to talk culture and get drunk on beer."

"Ha! That sounds more like you."

"You ready?" said Frank.

"*Vamos,*" said Hector, and they went down the stairs and out into the massive crowds.

Every year it was the same. It never changed. The sheer physicality of the *fiesta*, the waves of energy that swept over him as he walked over the cobblestone streets that he had seen so many times before.

He looked at his watch. It was 5:20. Time to pick up the tempo. He didn't want to be late for this meeting. The psychiatrist was indeed an admirer of his poetry and had found Frank on Facebook. Which in itself was unusual. Not because he was hard to find, quite the opposite. What was strange was that his poetry was virtually unknown outside of his family and his publisher and yet this guy had looked him up.

"Yo, Frank, how 'bout we stop somewhere and get something to drink for the road, it's hot out here."

"*Abbiamo l'imbarazzo della scelta,*" said Frank.

"What's that?"

"Italian, and it means roughly that there are so many goddamned bars in this town that all you got to do is choose, brother."

"There's one," said Hector, pointing to the bar on the corner of Calle de la Navarrería.

"Perfect," said Frank, and they walked in, asked for two Vodka tonics, looked at the three young ladies to their right who were wearing sangria stained t-shirts, paid the barman for their drinks and left.

Café Iruña was packed but they found a table out in the sun and sat down and waited for the Russian to show up. Anton Bukharin arrived at five thirty-six with three of his friends. He was significantly younger than Frank had imagined him to be and was sporting a mustache and a goatee. He had light skin, brown eyes and a smile that put you immediately at ease.

"Frank," he said, holding out his hand, "finally we get to see each other in person!"

"I was wondering if we ever would, but then I thought, everything that's destined to happen happens during the *fiesta*."

"Indeed it does, my friend."

"Oh, and this is Hector," said Frank, "a fellow writer friend."

"*Encantado*." said Anton. "Are you a poet?"

"No, I write fiction."

"Interesting, and you come here to the *fiesta* for inspiration?"

"Every year," said Hector, "and you work as a therapist, I've heard."

"More on the clinical side."

"How's that?"

"In a hospital," Anton told him with a mischievous grin, "with the crazies."

"Nice," said Hector.

"And these are my friends, Jaime, Maria and Irina," said Anton, indicating the three people who were standing next to him.

Jaime was tall and thin and looked very Spanish, or Navarrese or Basque, in short, someone from Pamplona. The women were Russian

14

and both Frank and Hector couldn't stop looking at them, in particular the redhead. Frank knew that it wasn't polite to stare, and he tried to look away at Anton or Jaime, but it was no use. Irina was very pretty, but it wasn't just her beauty. She was dangerously attractive and he reminded himself that she had to be at least twenty years younger than he was and absolutely out of his league. Girls like her didn't hang around forty-something poets, especially when they were unknown, and yet he had never seen anyone like her and thought that it was, perhaps, true what they said about Russian women. That maybe he had wasted his best years in the States and Italy and that if he could do it all again he would have told his parents to leave California, would have told them that from the womb, and would have made them promise to have him in Moscow, Saint Petersburg, Irkutsk, Omsk, wherever, it didn't matter, just so long as it was in Russia.

"Hey Frank, I'm gonna go get some cigies at the bar, be right back. If you guys are ordering get me one of what everyone else is having, and don't pay for it, the first round is on me."

"Thanks, man."

As soon as Hector was gone, Frank had a good look at his newfound acquaintances, realized that he didn't really know any of these people and thought, who cares, it's *fiesta*. He doubted seriously that he would ever meet anyone in the future as hot as the woman who was sitting across from him. Which, of course, didn't make any sense at all because the world was full of beautiful women everywhere you looked, but none of them up to now had ever hit him with such force. There was something chemical going on here, it was as if their

15

pheromones had met, talked it over, and decided on their own that there were no two ways about it, Frank and Irina were perfect for each other and that, as far as the pheromones were concerned, they might as well skip the formalities and start making babies as soon as possible. It was that proverbial struck by lightning feeling, with attendant butterflies in his stomach and blushing cheeks. What he felt was that he had been given another chance with the young Russian and all he could think about was Irina and how he might talk to her without being too obvious and yet knowing that sooner or later he would say something stupid and that there was nothing he could do about that.

"So the two of you are an item?" he asked as casually as he could, when what he intended to say was more along the lines of "Are the two of you good friends?" but not just good friends but good friends and other things that he would have included in that sentence to give the idea that he was only interested in her name, place of birth and perhaps her favorite color or wine. Not that he had been irretrievably smitten by her beauty or that in fact he was asking if she was available.

"A moment," said Irina and she whispered something to the other Russian woman who laughed and whispered something back.

"No, we're not. Just friends," she said, and Frank felt a slight tremor in his chest and he asked her many other questions, none of which he could remember the next day. The only thing that he could recall, and that was because Irina had written it on a piece of paper, was the name of the Basque bar where they had agreed to meet later on that night.

16

When Hector returned with his usual boyish smile and holding a pack of Marlboros, he sat down and then flagged down a waiter to order another round of beers.

"There were a lot of people in the bar," he said by way of apology. "Sorry it took me so long. Did I miss anything?"

"We were just chatting," said Frank.

"So where are you from?" said Irina to Hector.

"San Diego," he told her. "You ever been there?"

"Never," said Irina.

"That's too bad," said Hector.

"Why?" she asked.

"It's a pretty city, but if you're ever there, let me know. You can stay at my place."

"Thank you," said Irina, smiling, and Frank thought that afterwards he would have to have a talk with Hector and ask him just what the hell he thought he was doing hitting up on Irina like that.

Later when everyone had finished their beers Anton said that he had to go, and Maria, Jaime and Irina got up to leave with him.

"It's been a real pleasure," said Anton, "we should stay in touch."

"It was great meeting you," Frank told him, thinking that he would probably see him anyway in a couple of hours at the Basque bar, but then again he might not.

The locals had a saying for it, *La fiesta está por la calle*, which literally translated meant that the party is in the streets, but it also emphasized the spontaneity of San Fermin and the fact that you never

17

knew who you might run into from one minute to the next. Appointments made were often broken because everyone's plans were continuously changing. You could bump into an old friend, agree to meet at some restaurant after the bullfights and then later you might meet someone else, perhaps someone who you'd never seen before and the two of you or the two of you and the group that you had joined would wander off to another restaurant or bar and the plans that you had made before were forgotten and no one took it badly. It was just the way things were during the *fiesta*.

Frank kept an eye on Anton's group as they moved away from the table and out into the crowd. Irina was the last of them to disappear from view and just before she did he saw her looking back at him, or at least he thought that was what she was doing, because for all he knew she could have been looking at Hector.

The *Fiesta de San Fermín* was certainly wild and unpredictable but there were also things that you could count on. If, for instance, you wanted someone to disappear from your life then disappear they would. With close to a million people wandering the streets, laughing and drinking and partying like there was no tomorrow, and all of them dressed in identical red and white, everyone's anonymity, including Frank's, was more than guaranteed. But the same could also be said for Irina. If, for some reason, she changed her mind about Frank then that would be the end of that. No more pheromones, or butterflies or anything of that sort. It would be as if he'd never met her, a real dead end.

To chase away these pessimistic thoughts and to quell the rumbling of his stomach he walked up Calle Estafeta with Hector until they found a tavern where they ordered a plate of *Jamon Iberico* and two pints of beer. The Russian could be anywhere in this town, he thought, and anything could and usually did happen in Pamplona during the *fiesta*. But he would find her, he told himself. He knew where they would meet and when. All he had to do was believe that she would be there.

Chapter 3

It was the night before San Fermin, Pamplona's patron saint, and in front of Bar Zurika a Basque heavy metal band was playing their repertoire of politically inspired fight songs. The music was deafening and the crowd was very young and very drunk. Most of them had been drinking for at least the last ten hours and they would dance and party until five or six in the morning when a good number of them would crash where they stood, in gutters, on doorsteps, park benches, wherever it was that they ran out of gas. While the more energetic would manage to stay awake until sunrise and take their chances in the *encierro*.

Frank spotted Irina in the middle of the mosh pit of dancers. Her bright red hair set her apart from the others and she had a style when she moved that was both physically seductive and subconsciously addictive. Her dancing spoke of freedom and the promise or illusion of connection while still maintaining a discreet distance between herself and her many male and female fans.

When the band took a break Frank saw his chance and pushed his way through the crowd until he was close enough to tap her on the shoulder.

"Irina," he said and she turned around and looked at him with her green eyes and smiled.

"I was waiting for you."

"Looked to me like you were dancing," said Frank.

"Do you like to dance?"

"Sure, but only when I've had too much to drink."

"Well, then let's go inside and get you started."

He walked behind her and thought that in spite of her youth everything about her reminded him of another age, of an elegance and poise that was hard to find these days. She made him think, even with her sangria stained white trousers and t-shirt, of a femme fatale from the nineteen forties. There was something blue steel and yet very feminine about her. Something that had a noir feel to it, sultry and provocative and so out of tune with these puritanical times. She was a gift from the past, sent to remind us of how far we had fallen. Impossible to believe and yet there she was.

At the bar Frank asked for a *caña* but she corrected his request and told the bartender to give them two Vodka tonics.

"You're wasting your time with beer," she said, and kissed him on the lips.

"Aye aye, captain."

"We've got a lot of ground to cover before the sun rises."

"Have you got a plan?"

"Absolutely. First I get you drunk and then you do what I want you to do."

"Sounds reasonable," he said, as the bartender gave them their Vodka tonics.

"*Doce euros*," said the bartender and Frank pulled out a twenty-euro note and handed it to him.

"You're a rich man, Mister. Do you have a last name?"

"You still remember my first name?"

"Another five of these and I might forget, that's why I'll need to know your last name."

"Ardito," he said.

"Funny name, Frank Ardito. What does it mean?"

"Courageous, bold, daring, brave, something along those lines, I think."

"You take chances?"

"I might."

"To bold men," she said, raising her glass, "who take what they want, whenever they want it."

"To bold men," he agreed.

"And no toast to the drunken shrinks?!" shouted a voice behind them.

"Anton!" said Irina. "Where were you?"

"I was here, in the back, but with all these people who the hell knows where anyone is. Listen," he told the bartender, "give me two of what they're having. No, make that four, two for me and refills for them."

"*Cuatro Vodka tonic*," said the bartender to the girl who was helping him.

"*Muy bien*," said Anton. "Now what I want to know is, are the two of you ready for San Fermin?"

"We're here," said Frank, "what's the rush?"

"No rush but we have to get from here to there," he said, gesturing to a point somewhere outside the bar.

"Even if we're already here?"

"Even if we're already here. We'll still have to cross the long hours from now to when the bulls are let out of their pens at 8 a.m., and it won't be easy. There will be many people and bars and debauchery."

"Sounds like my kind of night."

"And you will be tempted."

"To do what?"

"To let sleep get the better of you."

"Possibly, but do you have a plan?"

"I'm a psychiatrist," said Anton, "I like to feel my way into things. No plans!"

So they toasted to Anton's lack of planning and to many other things that they could wish for or might want to fix, such as a sovereign Basque homeland and an indivisible Republican Spain with Don Felipe VI, Doña Letizia and the *Infantas* as tax paying citizens, plus Chupa Chupas, Vladimir Putin, Donald Trump, the USA and all the lovely Russians and their collusive ways.

When they finally finished with the toasts and their drinks they left the Zurika and wandered through the old town, bar hopping as they went.

Chapter 4

At Bar Txoko the crowd was spilling out onto the sidewalk and people were dancing with cigarettes and drinks in their hands to a mix of techno and dub-step. It was two in the morning and everywhere Frank looked the bars were open for business with no end in sight to the money that they were raking in and no worries about the sun that would eventually rise.

To his right Anton was trying to convince a Spanish woman to come away with him to another bar while outside Irina was being chatted up in broken English and French by two Africans who with the excuse of trying to sell her a wrist band were slowly moving her away from the table where she had been sitting. Frank was waiting to be served and checking from time to time on the progress of the Africans. They were good at what they did for a living and she was drunk enough to admit with her smiles and the look in her eyes that she appreciated the attention, and Frank thought that if the bartender didn't come soon she would probably slip away with them. Normally he would have immediately ditched the drinks and shooed the Africans away to claim what was his but he was pissed to the point where he felt strangely torn at having to choose between her or the refreshments. After all, she was the one who'd ordered the drinks.

At another bar she had confided in him that back in St. Petersburg she was a "professional alcoholic", in the sense that she drank for a living. She worked for a company that imported alcohol from the E.U. and every day there was always an open bottle or two at her desk. She was trained as a sommelier and it was her responsibility to "quality control" the latest arrivals before they were sent out to the stores.

What she hadn't confided in Frank was that from the beginning, even before he had said anything to her, she had sensed his "power" and this, for Irina, was very important. It had nothing to do with his physical strength or his wealth or lack of it. She recognized it as more of an animal attraction than anything else and where she came from it was usually indicative of a strong masculine personality. It wasn't the first time that she had sensed this in a man nor was it especially a guarantee of ultimate compatibility, but it was a start and she trusted her instincts.

When the bartender finally handed the two Vodka tonics to someone else Frank gave up on the drinks and walked outside to rescue Irina from the Africans. He had waited long enough.

"You seem to have friends wherever we go," he told her, as he took her by the hand and steered her back towards the bar.

"Who?" she asked.

"The Africans."

"Those two?" she said, blowing them both a kiss.

"Yes."

"Oh, they were very sweet and wanted me to go for a walk with them, to another locale or something, I can't remember."

"I bet they did."

Back inside Txoko Anton was waiting for them at the bar with two more Vodka tonics.

"Look what I found," he said, "one for each of you."

"*Gracias, amigo!*"

"*Hombre, de nada.*"

"So what happened to your *señorita*?" asked Frank.

"She had a boyfriend."

"Who was with her?"

"Yes."

"There while you were chatting her up?"

"*Claro.*"

"And you let that stop you?"

"It was slightly problematic, don't you think?"

"Nonsense, you should have invited him along."

"The three of us?" said Anton.

"Absolutely, and in a few days after drinking and running with the bulls and eating with the *peñas* and doing pretty much everything together if you and she decided to get married then he could be your best man," said Frank.

"You're drunk."

"I am but I'm dead serious, you know how difficult it is to find a really good best man?"

"No, I have no idea. How difficult is it?"

"Damn near impossible, *amigo*. That's how difficult. But not only have you found an absolutely valid future *señora* you've already located your really good best man for the wedding."

"Game, set, and match," said the psychiatrist.

"*Hombre*, you're way ahead of the curve, believe me."

Frank guessed that they would be ready to move off to another bar soon. His Russian friends were restless, and as their self-appointed guide he knew exactly where they needed to go.

Bar Windsor was right next to Hotel La Perla where Hemingway had stayed and where rumor had it that they charged upwards of a thousand six hundred euros a night during the *fiesta* to those *aficionados* of the author who absolutely had to do everything and be everywhere Hemingway had been, which in this case was the room where he had slept.

Frank himself was not a great fan of Ernest Hemingway. He had read him, of course, and as a writer he respected his talent but his tastes in literature lay elsewhere. Joyce or Fitzgerald were the writers that came to mind when he thought of that period, not Hemingway, but this was Pamplona, a town that he pretty much single-handedly put on the map with his novel *The Sun Also Rises*.

People came to the *fiesta* for a variety of reasons. Some came for the drinking, others for the camaraderie and the encounters, while others still were only there to run with the bulls, punctually risking their lives every morning at eight for an adrenaline fix that lasted no more than five to fifteen seconds at the max. Hemingway, to his credit, had come for all of these reasons although word has it that he never ran with the bulls. He understood and embraced the *fiesta* and in particular the *encierro*. Running with the bulls helped a man come to terms with the fact that nothing was permanent in life. Death, as Frank once heard a matador say, surrounded us all and Spain was one of the few places left on the planet that actually let you experience this truth without airbags, insurance, helmets or other encumbrances. It was just you and a herd of enraged half-ton bulls.

As they approached the Windsor, Frank thought that he could see one of his friends, shouting to him and waving a pint of beer in the air.

"There's our next stop," said Frank to Irina and Anton. He recognized the people at the table. Ian Hamilton, the one who had waved a beer at him, was a Scottish hipster from Edinburgh who worked on derivatives for a brokerage firm in the City. He had a Ph.D., a long beard decorated with red and black beads and shoulder-length grayish blonde hair shaved close on the sides, all of which gave him the appearance of a Viking or a Druid priest. Sitting next to him was Clive, a British *novillero* who before he'd seen the light and taken up bullfighting had been an animal rights activist. Peter was an ex-Navy Seal who had deployed to Afghanistan and who had discovered that running with the bulls was just about the only thing that helped him cope with his PTSD. And finally there was Hector, his roommate and best friend and a one-time Golden Gloves contender out of San Diego who never went pro on account of his bipolar disorder. He also ran. Said it kept him sane and was better than Lithium, although he took that too, just in case.

"Ardito, you wanker!" said Ian by way of a greeting.

"Ian," said Frank, shaking his hand, "good to see you haven't changed much."

"You should never mess with perfection, Ardito, didn't I teach you that?"

28

"Never," said Frank, as he introduced Irina and Anton to the others.

"Ardito has definitely upped his game this year," said Ian, taking a long look at Irina.

"Didn't think I had it in me, did ya?"

"A wanker like you? Are you kidding?" said Ian, giving Frank a friendly slap on the back. "Beers for the three of you?"

"You're offering?"

"No, Clive is," said Ian.

"I am?" said Clive.

"You are," and he passed Clive a twenty-euro note. "Next round is on you," he told Frank.

"Thanks."

"Thank you in advance," said Ian with a smile, and then, "So tell me how long have the two of you been going out?"

"Since this afternoon, no?" said Frank, glancing at Irina.

"What's *going out*?" asked Irina, pretending that she had never heard the phrase before.

"Good question," said Ian, "that's when not only does he buy you your drinks but he shags you as well." Peter and Hector laughed, but Frank was waiting to see what Irina thought. Ian had a preference for off-color, in your face comments and while for him it was a normal way of breaking the ice not everyone appreciated his sense of humor.

"What is *to shag*?" she asked.

Frank whispered into her ear and Irina laughed and said, "No, we have not shagged, not yet, but the night is long."

29

"And the *fiesta* longer still!" added Ian.

The conversation then shifted to the *encierro*. Hector asked Ian if he was going to run where he usually ran from the top of Estafeta down into the bullring or if he wanted to take a chance on the *curva*.

"What's the *curva*?" asked Irina.

"A place where you probably wouldn't want to be," said Frank.

"Why not?"

"It's a bit like painting a bullseye on yourself, especially if you're standing against the barrier on the left side," said Clive.

"And where do you run?" Irina asked Clive.

"Sometimes on the *curva*, sometimes further up Estafeta, it depends."

Frank liked Clive even though they didn't have much in common. Clive came from a well to do family of London bankers and aristocrats, while Frank's father had sold Subarus in the San Fernando Valley. Initially Clive was set on following his father into the world of finance. It was the path of least resistance, a cush job with plenty of perks. He couldn't have asked for more. His father would be happy, his mother would be happy, everyone would be happy but that is not what he did. By chance he saw a squadron of Tornadoes flying low in close formation up in the Scottish Highlands. They moved with such precision and power that he decided then and there that to fly like that, the way they did it, would be something much more than a career. It was a romantic vision of his freedom, shooting across the skies at twice the speed of sound. Patriotism really had nothing to do with his choice. "Fuck the regime" had always been his motto. He just wanted to fly, to be up there and not down here. A few weeks later, when he'd graduated from university with a degree in economics, he reported to his commanding officer at RAF Hemswell for flight training.

Clive was without a doubt their most promising pilot, one of the best that they had had in years. His instinctive ability never ceased to amaze his instructors. Nothing ever went wrong when Clive was in command. Until, that is, the day that it did.

His objective the morning of the incident was to avoid radar detection by flipping the plane belly up just before he approached a hill so that it wouldn't balloon excessively and reveal his position. He executed the maneuver perfectly. Then while he was flying the Tornado upside down the engines cut out forcing him to eject. First the gyros in the seat pushed him down and out and then straight up. The combined g-forces of the U-turn ejection left him in a state of shock when his parachute hit the ground. He hadn't broken anything but he didn't know where he was or what had happened to his plane so he started walking. That was what they had trained him to do, to walk it off. When they finally found him and took him back to the base he had been missing for three days and was officially AWOL. Technically that was true, he had been wandering about the English countryside without permission, but it wasn't his fault. The Tornado's RB.199 power plant was to blame and, as a result, he now had a black mark on an otherwise perfect service record. For Clive just the idea that they could even consider him Absent Without Leave was an insult to his personal code of ethics and the more he thought about it the more it rubbed him the wrong way. When he decided to quit and resigned his commission initially they had no intention of letting him out. Training a fighter pilot was exceedingly expensive and they wanted to nail his ass. This was towards the tail end of the Cold War and they accused him of having pro-Russian sympathies and of being a closet communist. He said that he had never met a Russian in his life and that he wasn't a leftist. They then asked him what he thought about nuclear war and would he be willing to bomb the Soviets to defend the Royal family. He said that, as an officer, he had to obey his superiors. He didn't tell them what he thought about the Royals or waging nuclear war. The Royals simply weren't worth protecting and World War III was unwinnable. It would be the end of everything and he wasn't about to go down in the history books (if any were ever written) as the guy who dropped the first bomb. He just signed the piece of paper they handed him, saluted, left the base and didn't look back.

On a lighter side Clive and Frank were about the same age with Clive being a few years older. Clive was also taller and more muscular thanks to his sports and his bullfighting.

"Do you think you'll run in the morning?" Clive asked Irina.

"I might if I don't fall asleep before then," she said.

"Stick with us," said Hector, "we'll keep you awake."

"Awake and hydrated!" said Ian, lifting his mug to the idea of Irina running.

"Have any women ever been gored?" she asked.

"Probably," said Frank.

"About three," said Peter, looking up from his beer. "The last time was about six years ago. A young Australian woman got it in the back from a Miura. Broke a rib and punctured her lung."

"So the odds of you finishing your run without a scratch are good," said Clive.

"Statistically you're in like Flynn," said Ian.

"Not too many women run?" she asked.

"Nope, it's largely a male preserve," said Frank.

"Which is why having you run with us is special," said Clive.

"I didn't say that I would definitely run! I said that I might."

"Of course you will, my dear," Ian reassured her. "Nothing to fear."

He also said that because she was young and slim and had deliciously long legs her run would undoubtedly be swift and sure.

"Deliciously long?" said Frank.

"You disagree?"

"No, I was just marveling at your acute powers of observation."

"Me thinks your boyfriend is a jealous man," said Ian to Irina.

"He might be," said Irina and she kissed Frank deeply.

When she came up for air she declared, holding her half-emptied pint, "We need something stronger than this!"

"Wodka?" said Anton who had been thinking the same thing.

"Vodka," she agreed. "A Vodka tonic. Where's the waiter?"

"You have to go inside," said Ian.

"I'll get 'em," said Frank. His chair was closest to the bar and he felt like stretching his legs. Inside, of course, it was packed to the

33

rafters and again he had to literally squeeze his way to a spot where the bartender could finally see him and take his order. The struggle to get there reminded him of the time a few years back when he had hooked up with a German in front of the *Ayutamiento* during the *Chupinazo* (the opening ceremony of the *fiesta*). Her name was Anna Schmidt and she was a businesswoman in her late thirties who had flown down from Frankfurt on a whim because she had just found out about San Fermin and thought that Pamplona would be the ideal place to meet a young Mandingo who could knock her up for free. She was fast running down her fertility clock but like most sociopathic executives she had a plan for any contingency. She was going to have a baby, by God, even if it killed her. She would beat back the hands of time. The only problem, as Frank could see it, was that she was psychologically ill adapted to the rigors of the *fiesta*. Physically she was in shape and an alcoholic to boot, which was certainly a plus in a town that was literally swimming in booze, but mentally she was a control freak and that was about as bad as it could get for anyone who hoped not only to survive but also to thrive during the nine days of the *fiesta*.

Anna objected to everything and everyone, categorically. Nothing met with her approval. The people were too loud. The *peña* bands were horrible. The trash was everywhere and covered the cobblestones of the *Casco Viejo* in a layer of crushed plastic cups. The smells were oppressive to her delicate nose, the stale beer, the piss and the vomit, the sweat and all the other things that she couldn't even begin to name. The town and its filthy party were an assault on her fragile equilibrium. She couldn't control it. She could not exterminate

34

its pagan soul and the more she understood this the more she began to panic. She finally reached her breaking point at half past two in the morning of the seventh. Covered in sangria and looking at Frank with dilated eyes and her face drained of any color she told him, "I have to get out of here. I have to get out of here now!" and she found a man who for the outrageous price of 500 euros agreed to drive her the one hundred and fifty-five kilometers to the airport in Bilbao.

At least, thought Frank, he wouldn't have to worry about Irina abandoning ship. She was cut from an altogether different cloth. Born just two years after the collapse of the USSR she had grown up in an age of disaster capitalism where only the strongest survived and the weak disappeared anonymously in forgotten Stalinist apartments of the once triumphant working class. No, Irina took nothing for granted and was determined to live her life to the fullest, come what may.

On his way back to the table with the Vodka tonics Frank saw that Hector was pestering Peter yet again about his war wound. Peter had been shot in his right shoulder blade when he and his platoon were pinned down by enemy fire thirty miles southwest of Khost near the Pakistani border. Hector wanted to know what it felt like and was trying to compare Peter's experience to his own "battle wound", as he called it, which in fact had nothing to do with battles or war. He had been gored the year before in his right buttock and never lost the opportunity to talk about it, be it with his friends or journalists or random people who he met at the *fiesta*. It was his souvenir, a little hole that filled him with joy. So charged was he by this experience that occasionally when he'd had too much to drink, in a bar or out in the street, he would drop his pants and let the curious see his wound for themselves, actually let them touch the spot where the bull's horn had punctured his flesh. He noticed that not only did the girls get a kick out of feeling him down there but even a few men would take the opportunity to investigate. Still, in the back of his mind there was this nagging suspicion that a bullet wound taken in a real battle was worth twice as much as a *toro bravo* poking you in the ass in Pamplona in terms of bragging rights. Hence the many conversations he had with Peter.

"You keep telling everybody that it was no big deal," said Hector.

"Actually, you're the one who likes to talk about big deals," said Peter, grinning and wondering how many more beers it would take before Hector went ballistic and flashed his Chicano *martillo de Thor*.

"Be honest."

"About what?"

"Tell us today, because you didn't tell us last year or the year before that what it really felt like."

"Didn't feel like anything, really."

"I'm serious, Peter."

"Like someone was just tapping me on the shoulder."

"*Pendejo*, can't you just come out with it?"

"Like a friend was behind me and trying to get my attention. You know how insistent friends can be," said Peter with a wink.

"It knocked you down, didn't it? Blew a hole right though your shoulder blade."

"Nothing of the sort, my dear Hector. It was a caress, quiet and gentle."

"Caress, my ass."

"Speaking of which, is anyone ready for another drink?" asked Ian.

"My round," said Frank.

"Where are you going?" said Ian.

"To the bar."

"They have waiters here, you know."

"Now you tell me."

"Didn't want to make it too easy for you."

"Of course not."

"There's only so much good fortune that a man is entitled to in one day," said Ian, glancing at Irina to drive home his point. "And you, Frank, have greatly exceeded your limit."

"Ian," said Clive, "stop trying to hit up on Ardito's new flame."

"Yeah," said Peter, "he's only just met her. Slack off."

"Who said I was hitting up on her?"

"Clive did," said Hector.

"Well, he's right," said Ian. "I admit it, I was, but only because I believe that Frank is a lucky fucking wanker and that he needs to be reminded of this from time to time. For his own good."

"I'll drink to that," said Hector, raising an empty plastic cup.

Ian flagged down the waiter and more drinks were brought to their table.

"How late is this place open?" asked Irina.

"I imagine we've got another couple of hours, if you're up to it," said Peter.

"We're Russian," she said, putting her arm over Anton's shoulders. "This is nothing for us."

Peter smiled and raised his beer mug in her direction. Hector reminded his friend that he was still waiting for an answer.

"I already told you," said Peter.

"I want the truth."

"A caress," he said.

"The truth," Hector repeated, as he stood up on his chair.

"Clive," said Ian, and Clive understood and nodded.

"A gentle caress, my friend," said Peter and Frank could feel the tension in the air. The others had been through this many times before and they knew what to do whenever Hector felt the need to publicly reaffirm his values.

"I just asked you a simple question," Hector told him.

"A gentle caress," Peter patiently repeated.

"What is it about you that fails to see what I'm getting at, that fails to see the connection between our experiences? It really isn't so hard to understand, is it? You and I are both heroes and we risked our lives to discover the fundamental necessity of our passions, you in fucking Afghanistan and me here with the bulls. Neither of us is better than the other, we are the same man. We are brothers and just because I got mine in the ass does not mean that I love you in a carnal way. I am not a faggot, Peter!", and Ian turned to Frank and whispered, "Wait for it."

38

"You won't show me your wound, Peter, but I will show you mine because I am not ashamed and I love you, brother!"

"Clive," said Ian, and both Clive and Peter sprang into action, but it was too late. Hector had already dropped his white trousers and his underwear and was standing there on his chair with this enormous erection, shouting at the top of his lungs, "Come and feel it, bitches! Touch my battle scar and weep, cause there ain't none of you, except Peter and Peter's shy, that comes close!"

"Get him!" said Ian, and Clive and Peter, laughing hysterically, pulled him off the chair and wrestled him onto the ground. They were both strong men but Hector was built like a rock and throwing punches.

"Why the fuck does he always have to hit us?" said Peter.

"Cause he's in his berserker mode," Clive told him, dodging Hector's fists.

"Hurry up and get his pants back on, forget about the underwear!" said Ian. The local police would be there soon and it was important to have Hector dressed when they arrived if they didn't want their friend to spend the rest of the night in jail and miss the first *encierro*. He was certifiably insane, there was no doubt about it, but they all agreed that that had never been a good reason to keep a man from running with the bulls.

Chapter 5

At four o'clock they were finally alone. Frank walked with Irina up to the Cathedral in Plaza de San José where she knocked repeatedly on one of the side entrances, saying that if God was real and the priests were there then they would let her in. But the priests didn't open the door and she started to taunt them in English and in the little Spanish that she knew.

"*Oye*! I know that you're in there, *maricones*! Come out, come out, wherever you are, the jig is up!"

"The jig is up? You've been watching too many gangster films," Frank told her, laughing.

"Am I wrong? Is there something wrong with my syntax? Are you criticizing my English?" she asked, banging on the thick and very heavy looking wooden doors.

"Not at all, you're English is wonderful."

"Then why don't these *hijos de puta* answer?!"

"That's a good question," said Frank, laughing. "Perhaps they're sleeping."

"Or shagging!" she said, giving the doors a good kick.

"Or out drinking?" suggested Frank. "Incognito, of course."

"Incognito?"

"No frocks, just red and white, like everyone else, but with Catholic *pañuelos,* dipped in holy water."

"Fuck that!" she shouted at the doors. "I want them to come out and I want them to come out now!"

40

"Doesn't look like they're listening."

"Cowards!" she screamed and then laughed. "*Cobardes maricones!*"

"Do you feel better now? Did you get it out of your system?"

"Much better!" she exclaimed, and while she was still very drunk she stopped banging on the doors of the Cathedral and gave up all hope of ever seeing the priests or their savior.

"Let's go," he said and she took his hand and they walked to the stone building where he and Hector had their small apartment with a view of the town, the river and the mountains to the north.

Chapter 6

Irina passed out in front of the main entrance. Coming over from the Cathedral Frank had thought about taking her upstairs to his room and what it would be like to sleep with her, but apparently that was not to be. Not tonight at any rate. He couldn't take her back to her hotel because he had no idea where she was staying, and so he carried her up the four flights of stairs slung over his right shoulder. She was relatively light but just the same his arm ached when he got to the top and laid her down on the floor while he looked for his key.

Walking inside he could see that Hector hadn't come back and that this being the night before the first run there was a good chance that he'd be out dancing and drinking until five or six in the morning.

He took Irina's shoes off and put a pillow under her head. Then he stood back and looked at her. He decided to take her clothes off and as he did he caressed her body. She was out cold. He could have done anything to her, but he didn't. Then he covered her up to her neck with a clean sheet and kissed her on her lips. Before closing the door to the bedroom he thought that perhaps he should leave a short message in case she woke up before he got back from the run, and then he looked at her again on the bed, as beautiful as ever and breathing softly, and guessed that she wouldn't be up before three or four in the afternoon.

He made himself comfortable on the couch and, as he closed his eyes, he could still hear her laughing at the priests. She was quite the character and he told himself that the sixth of July henceforth would be a day to remember, the day that he had met Irina from St. Petersburg.

42

His life, he felt, after a string of failed relationships had finally taken a turn for the better. There was something about her, something that he couldn't quite explain that told him that things had changed and that perhaps he had changed, too.

At six thirty he was already awake with a clean shirt and a splash of water on his face. He had slept about an hour and a half, an hour and forty-five minutes and that wasn't bad for the first night of the *fiesta*. He knew that many who were going to run today would not have slept at all and so he considered himself fortunate, as he locked the door to his apartment.

He was meeting Ian and the others at Estafeta 27. They had a large flat on the sixth floor, which they used as a way of circumventing the new system that corralled all the runners into the first half of the course from the pen at the beginning of Santo Domingo where the bulls were kept all the way up to the City Hall.

The city government had decided that enough was enough and that too many tourists had been running in the *encierros* without being fully aware of the dangers they faced. The *toro bravos* were big, agile and utterly untamed. They could throw a man in the air with a flick of their horns the way someone might casually toss a ballpoint pen to a friend. They did not know fear and when they ran all they wanted to do was to stick with the herd. When they were together they didn't care about the runners surrounding them, so long as the humans kept their distance. Nasty things happened when you got too close or when a bull was separated from the herd. A lone bull, or a *suelto* as he is called in Spanish, will immediately try to stake out his territory and if you happen to be within the striking radius of his horns he will do his best to kill you or to put you in the hospital with serious injuries. Frank had seen more than his fair share of gorings in all the years that he'd been coming to the *fiesta*. Runners could get it in the back, in their lungs, in their intestines, in their legs and even, as Hector had discovered, right in the ass.

There was even a case of a young Kiwi, twenty-two years old, running for the first time, in his first *fiesta*, in shorts no less, who had the misfortune of encountering a *suelto* near the *curva* of Estafeta. The bull weighed about five hundred and eighty kilos and was supremely teed-off. As it lashed out at anything that moved, the young New Zealander at first tried to run away from the *toro*, but the *toro* wasn't going to let that happen. It caught the young man in his right thigh but the horn didn't go into the muscle. When the bull pulled its head back its horn ripped a right angle in the Kiwi's leg so that a large flap of his skin was completely separated from the yellow fatty tissue just below it. Being not more than four meters away from the New Zealander Frank saw everything and it was as if he and the other runners and the spectators in the balconies above them were being given a lesson in human anatomy. The bull had chosen his sacrificial lamb and was allowing everyone else to see the things that you normally never got to see unless you were a surgeon.

The Kiwi at that point started limping in the other direction away from the *curva* and towards a barrier, which he thought that he would be able to climb, flapping skin and all. The bull, however, pursued him and knocked him off the barrier and onto the ground where he repeatedly tried to gore the New Zealander with his horns. Eventually one of the first aid teams managed to pull him under the barrier and away from the enraged bull.

So, yes, Frank would never deny that the *encierro* could be brutal, unforgiving and dangerous and that under the new rules perhaps it wasn't such a bad idea that the newbies were forced to watch a film of these marauding bulls, as they waited for nearly an hour, packed like sardines behind the barriers in front of the *Ayuntamiento*. But the film was not going to save anyone from the *sueltos*. Frank was sure of that because the running of the bulls was an event where shit did happen, all the time. But at least the city government could now defend itself and say that they had warned everyone and that if a tourist really wanted to run and the gods of the Aurochs had singled them out for punishment that day then they had no one to blame but themselves.

Smiling at this example of Iberian paternalism, Frank pressed the button on the intercom of 27 Estafeta and upstairs someone opened the door for him.

"Here we go," he said, pumping his fist into the air. "Let the runs begin!"

There was seriously nothing that could even come close to San Fermin. He had seen the Carnival in Rio and the Mardi Gras in New Orleans and they were colorful and steeped in their own traditions but paled in comparison to what went on here. This was the party to beat all parties, the celebration that you simply had to experience at least once in your lifetime. But more than that, for Frank, it was his second home. The town that he always returned to and which had never disappointed him. Here he had friends, people who cared about him in a way that he found hard to describe. There was a camaraderie that you could feel, a love, fueled perhaps by the alcohol but genuine just the same. He had been coming to Pamplona for many years and the *fiesta* had changed him to the point where he couldn't remember who he had once been. All he knew was that this ancient celebration, this bacchanalia, had cured him of his post-modern ills and had made him whole. Or that's what he liked to tell himself. There were still some cracks in his emotional armor, stuff about his family that he tried not to think about and the *Fiesta de San Fermín* was the shovel that helped him bury those thoughts, temporarily at least.

At the top of the stairwell he knocked on the door immediately to his left and then walked in.

"Ardito, is that you?" shouted Ian.

"None other," he said, waving to the guys he could see at the end of the hall.

"Took you long enough."

"What d'ya mean? It's not even seven."

"Sure it is and we've been waiting for you. Figured you were getting in your last shag with that Slavic *señorita*."

"Something like that," answered Frank, as Clive handed him a cup of coffee and told him not to pay any attention to Ian.

"The poor dear hasn't been given his morning enema."

"Constipation, eh?" said Frank.

"Of the mind," added Peter, who was sinking deep into the center seat of the couch with a cup of coffee in his hand.

46

"Nothing that a good run can't make right," said Hector, who appeared fully recovered from his nudist berserker episode at the Windsor.

"You should know," said Ian.

"In fact, never felt better," replied Hector.

"Well, now that you've got two holes back there it's got to be a hell of a lot easier to drop anchor when you need to."

"Oh piss off, Ian, where's my coffee?"

"Now now now, mind your tongue, young man," Ian told him, as he passed Hector his steaming mug of coffee.

"Does anyone know what time it is?" asked Peter.

"Seven twenty-five," said Frank.

"Find TVE on the telly," said Ian.

"Got it," said Hector.

"What are they saying? Translate for me."

"Not much. They're interviewing someone from the regional government, about the number of tourists this year, how everyone's happy with the turnout, bla, bla, bla. Usual crap."

"Yeah, they should get you on there, Hector, and you could tell 'em about your two holes."

"You're just jealous."

"Seriously, I think you'd be a hit, especially with that pretty blond journalist."

"Ian, you got any newspapers?" asked Peter.

"Yeah, look under the table."

Peter picked up yesterday's edition of El Pais and Diario de Navarra and placed them both on top of the table. It was time for everyone to roll a few sheets together to make a baton that they could use to either distract a bull or to measure the distance between themselves and a bull's horns. Many of those who had run for years and who knew what they were doing used them. They came in handy.

Ian liked to tell the story of the time he had started his run at the top of Estafeta, and just as he was approaching the ramp that led to the *callejón,* or the passageway into the bullring, he saw a young Asian couple jogging hand in hand down the ramp as if it were a Sunday afternoon in a city park somewhere in Tokyo or Hong Kong. They looked relaxed and completely oblivious to the fact they were about to enter into one of the most dangerous sections of the course. In the *callejón* there was no safe refuge, no place where you could escape and if a bull caught you down there nine times out of ten he was going to make you wish you had never taken that flight to Spain. Ian was running on the left side close to the barrier and the Asian couple on the far right side when he heard someone behind him shout out *"Suelto!"* and indeed coming up fast from the rear was a seven hundred kilo Miura bull whose shoulder was about as tall as Ian was and whose horns were at least as long as his arms were outstretched. It was going to flatten the young couple and then rip them into Teriyaki beef strips or something worse. He reacted instinctively without thinking. Holding his baton out in his right hand he sped up so that he was eye to eye with the Miura and waving the rolled newspaper in its direction he managed to distract the bull for a few seconds and allow the Asians to exit the tunnel safely into the arena. When he came out of the *callejón* with the bull now in front of him and heading towards the corrals at the other end of the ring he stopped to catch his breath, to curse the Asians and to thank the *toro bravo* that had given him one of the best runs of his life and that would die later on that day.

"OK," said Hector, "they're opening up the barriers."

"That's our cue, gentlemen. Let's go!" and all of them filed out the door and down the six floors to the entrance hall.

"*Estamos listos?*" asked Hector.

"As ready as we'll ever be," said Clive.

"*Suerte!*" said Ian, wishing them all good luck.

"*Suerte*, Ian," said Hector and the others embraced and shook hands. It was their moment of bonding and also a counter-jinx against any *mala suerte* on the run because the *encierro* was the *encierro*.

"Here we go, lads, see you all at Bar Txoko for drinks," and Ian opened the door and the five of them disappeared into the crowd of runners who were moving up from the City Hall.

Peter and Hector went in the other direction. They were heading towards *la curva* because that was where they usually ran. In the *encierro* you had to choose where you wanted to meet the herd of bulls and steers because no one could run the entire course with them. They were simply too quick and agile, reaching speeds of thirty-five to forty kilometers an hour in the faster stretches.

While the two of them were good friends, in many ways they were very different in terms of their character and how they approached the *encierro*. Hector liked to begin his run at the intersection of

Mercaderes and Estafeta on the right side of the road. He felt that it was a good vantage point and a place that heightened his instinctual powers. He was a Chicano, a Mexican-American with the blood of Aztecs running in his veins and he believed in shamanism and the power of visions. As a boxer, there had been many times when he had to trust his visions if he wanted to win. Good luck was not something casual in life. It depended on the balance of forces in the spiritual world and even if most of his friends would say that, apart from his training and preparation, it was just a question of chance if you won or not he liked to think that there was something more to it than that.

But was Hector himself a shaman? Had he ever touched the ecstasy of a "Man of Knowledge"? He liked to think that he had, or rather that if he hadn't then he was certainly on the path to enlightenment. Religious or spiritual ecstasy could be experienced in many ways and if running with a herd of *toro bravos* was not exactly what came to mind when most people thought of shamanism that in itself did not negate the truth or the intensity of his experience. Whenever he ran with his "brother bulls", as he affectionately called them, he ceased to be just an average American struggling with his bipolar disorder and became something else entirely. Running in front of the bulls or anywhere in their vicinity he was infused with their power and at the same time was connected to a distant past when Paleolithic Europeans left their artwork on the caves of Lascaux and Altamira. The Spanish fighting bulls that Hector chased every morning of the *fiesta* were in fact the direct descendants of the Aurochs depicted in the charcoal and ochre tinted frescos of the caves. These early

Europeans were celebrating the hunt and the *encierro* was a sacred link to this activity and the beginnings of European art and culture.

Peter, on the other hand, had a much less exalted view of the run. The bulls were fucking insane, the tourists who ran and who didn't know what they were doing were idiots and he was there to seduce as many women as he could. Which, of course, would have been possible even without the runs given his past as a warrior and decorated hero in Afghanistan. Peter was of the opinion that even in these priggish times nothing, as far as he could tell, seemed to resonate deeper in the hearts of women than the sight of a young, fit veteran of America's imperial wars in temporary need of a dose of tender loving care. Slice it any way you wanted but to Peter the mythos of the highly trained and swole defender of the fatherland's female population was alive and well in the twenty-first century.

The runs, however, were a plus. No question about it. Participating in the *encierro* was a dangerous hobby and potentially a lethal one. When Peter courted a woman during the *fiesta*, either with a dinner and a rose, or just a bottle of sangria and a baguette the fact that in just a few hours he could be lying on the cobblestones of the course in a pool of his own blood made his dates appreciate even more the sex that they would have before his possible death. It was the ephemerality of the act and the fact that they might never see him again that gave their couplings such a bittersweet quality.

Having a history as a semi-pro boxer wasn't bad when it came to finding women, thought Peter, and even being bipolar was something that perhaps could be marketed as a plus in a one night stand, as in

51

"Hey, I'm a victim just like you". But this business of Hector's visions was a definite negative in Peter's opinion. There was no getting around that. It was off-putting to women who absolutely did not want to hear of his desire to become some sort of yoga master. As Peter saw it, they wanted his raw energy, his wild man persona, and Hector had plenty of that for the ladies of Pamplona.

Peter had told him to drop it, saying that he was wasting his time. He had insisted, even argued with Hector that if he really wanted to get laid then Nirvana was not the path that he should be taking. Flaunt what you've got and keep the rest under wraps was Peter's philosophy of life.

Hector to his credit could not be swayed by Peter's arguments and remained true to his values. As he saw it, his task as a shaman would always be to help others in their spiritual journey towards enlightenment.

At 7:57 there were only three minutes left before they would light the first rocket and the gates of the corral at the beginning of Santo Domingo would open. The terminators of the *encierro* were about to take center stage and it was time for Hector to wish his fellow runners good luck. He looked at the man standing next to him with a cell phone in his hand.

"*Suerte,*" said Hector. The man, dressed in white except for his shoes and *pañuelo* and who had had his hair shaved like a Marine, could not have been more than twenty-three.

Perhaps surprised to hear someone speaking to him, he grabbed Hector's forearm in a Roman clasp and said, "you too".

"Is this your first time?" he asked Hector.

"No, I've been at it for a number of years. And you?"

"First time," said the man.

"You want some good advice?"

"Sure."

"Remember the Golden rule, if you fall down stay down and don't move. The bulls will jump over you if they have to, so long as they're running with the herd."

"And if they aren't?"

"Then kiss your ass good-bye."

"What?"

"No, that was a joke. Cover your head and roll yourself up into a ball and don't move."

"That's it?"

"Yeah, and pray."

Then they heard the first rocket explode and soon after the second one, which meant that the herd was compact.

"A minute, tops, and they'll be here," he told the Marine, who had a USMC tattoo on his right forearm.

"The bulls?"

"That's right, so don't go until I tell you to. You understand?"

"Got it."

Soon the mass of people on Mercaderes began to move. There were still no bulls in sight, not even the steers, but the *valientes* or the brave ones, as they were ironically called, were running far ahead of the rest of the crowd and they were jeered and whistled at by the thousands

53

of spectators looking down from the balconies and the windows of the buildings on either side of the course.

After the brave ones came the first of the real runners with Peter among them wearing his signature black flannel shirt with the collar that had been ripped off by a bull's horn in another run two years ago.

"Wait for it," Hector shouted to the Marine.

"Now?"

"Wait!" and as the first *toro bravo* came barreling into the curve he saw his chance and shouted "Go!" The Marine took no more than three steps before he was almost immediately knocked down onto the cobblestones by a cream-colored bull with a dark brown spot just below its left horn.

Hector sprinted out diagonally from where he was standing through a maze of people and steers with his eye on the bull that was leading the herd. He was going to catch up to it and then, if all went well, he would test his luck running between its horns.

He was so close to the triad of fighting bulls at the front of the herd that he could smell the caked shit on their tails. There were people everywhere, falling down or dodging those who were already on the ground. He was looking for an opening and he found one. The lead bull tripped over a runner that had fallen in front of it and slipped back into the herd. The bull on its left, which Hector had been following, took its place and for five seconds Hector was the new left wing of the triad. He was running with the fingertips of his right hand touching the *morillo* of the lead bull. He was one with the *manada* and its energy pulsed through his veins. He felt religiously ecstatic and was thinking that this time he would make it all the way into the Arena. Good things were possible in the *encierro* if you believed. But someone pushed him from behind and just before he smashed his face against the cobblestones and blacked out he thought that he could see Irina with her long red hair and longer legs running with the bulls at Telefónica.

Chapter 7

Frank and Ian had a good run and finished against the barriers before the *callejón*. Afterwards for something to eat and a coffee before they hit Txoko and had their first serious drink of the new day the two of them doubled back through the crowds to a café on Estafeta where they knew the croissants were always fresh and the cappuccinos blistering hot. To catch the highlights and analysis of the *encierro* there were two televisions mounted above the bar that were always tuned to TVE or the local news station.

"There's Peter," said Ian, looking up at one of the TVs, as the bartender put their cappuccinos and croissants in front of them.

"*Cinco euros cincuenta*," he said.

"I got it," said Frank.

"Next one's on me," said Ian.

"Man, look at the size of those bulls."

"Good thing you didn't bring your new flame."

"She conked out," Frank told him.

"It happens."

"She's pretty good with the strong stuff but I guess everyone has their limits."

"And bang! Down goes Peter," said Ian, looking up at the TV.

"He'll be there at Txoko with maybe a bruise on his elbow. Nothing ever happens to Peter."

"Oh look, there's Hector," said Ian.

"Jesus Christ, what a dash!"

"The man's an animal, a beast. Hell of a run," agreed Ian.

"Oops, there he goes, down for the count."

"Too bad," said Ian. "Hey Frank, look!"

"What?"

"It's your Russian lady."

"Who?"

"Irina, dummy, look, red hair, everything, it's her and she's kicking ass with the bulls," said Ian admiringly.

"Holy shit."

"I thought you said she passed out?"

"She did, but I guess she got up again."

"I'm sure that was her, Frank, no doubts about it."

"No, I think you're right," said Frank, who was surprised and amazed that not only did she wake up but that she was able to find the City Hall and run the way she'd run.

She was young and in shape but absolutely inexperienced in the *encierro* and yet her run was flawless, as if she were one of those people who had an innate talent for the event and Frank had seen a number of them over the years. But the more he thought about it the more it seemed impossible. Innate talent be damned, someone had coached Irina. Someone who had been with her had told her what to do and what not to do, what to avoid and what to expect. Her guardian angel, whoever he was, had also given her a few pointers regarding the bulls. This was not luck. This was something you couldn't fake. Someone with intimate knowledge of the *toro bravo* had helped her with her run. But was that such a bad thing, thought Frank? If anything, he owed the guy a beer for keeping his girlfriend out of harm's way.

"Shall we go?" asked Ian.

"*Vámonos*," said Frank and they left the café, turned right and then right again until they reached the open window at Txoko that served the bar's version of an "Absolut Bitch", or a "Hemingway" as some referred to it, which was normally a shooter but they had extended it to make a cocktail. The "Bitch", as they affectionately called it was a mix of Absolut Vodka, Baileys Irish Cream, Tuaca and Kahlua. It was smooth and sweet and could calm anyone's nerves after a close call or a fall during the run.

"Cheers," said Ian, as he handed Frank his Bitch.

"Cheers," said Frank, "great way to start the day."

"And to many more like it!" said Ian, raising his glass.

"You know, I wonder where she went," said Frank.

"Right behind you, cowboy."

"What?"

"Standing over there with Clive." And Frank turned around and there she was with a group of other runners and the ex-fighter pilot.

"Well, that figures," said Frank, as he walked over to Irina. She was wearing the same pants that she'd had on yesterday although her shirt was different. Her hair was tied in a ponytail for the *encierro* and her cheeks were flushed red.

"Frank!" she said, giving him a kiss on the lips.

"Morning, beautiful."

"Did you see me running with the bulls?" she asked with a touch of pride in her voice.

"I saw you on the television, if that's what you mean."

"Where were you?"

"With Ian."

"Where are the others?" she said.

"Well, I see you found Clive," said Frank.

"No, he found me."

"Well, I'm not sure. I know that both Peter and Hector ran. They were on the TV, though Hector had a nasty fall. Wouldn't be surprised if they took him to the hospital."

"A brain scan would be useful," said Ian.

"That way we could finally find out if he has one," said Clive and everyone laughed.

The sanitation crews were still busy cleaning the Plaza with their trucks, water cannons and brooms. Every day to keep Pamplona from being literally buried in trash they collected mountains of crushed plastic cups, broken glass, paper, straws, condoms, wallets and whatever else they could find on the pavement or parks of the city. Where they put it all was anyone's guess but every morning by ten the Plaza looked almost as clean as it had been the day before the beginning of the *fiesta*.

A crew with a truck and its high-powered hose was moving towards the group and Frank took Irina's hand and sought refuge near the bar's outdoor seating.

"Here comes the cleansing flood," said Ian, "that washes away the sins and garbage of the world!"

"Something tells me they would need quite a few more trucks to clean all the sins of this town," said Frank.

"Sin?" said Clive. "No worries, *hombre*, they've all been forgiven. It's a Catholic party, you can do what you want here and even if what you want gets out of hand you can pay the church to clean up your mess and it'll be as if it never happened."

"Indulgences," said Ian.

"No wonder the church has lasted as long as it has," said Frank.

"Now that is a con I wish I had thought of," lamented Ian. "They must be raking it in."

"Ian, we're talking about the Middle Ages. They stopped their celestial pay 'n play scheme ages ago," said Frank.

"Well, not quite," Clive corrected him. "They're still doing it, except now it's called Charity."

"Sweet," said Frank.

"To the *fiesta*!" said Ian, raising his drink into the air.

"*A la fiesta*!" said the others, as they joined in his toast. The world was a fairly dysfunctional place most everyone there agreed, but life itself was still worth living if you could put it all behind you for nine days and drown your sorrows in the ancient traditions of this bacchanalia.

Peter showed up after the toast. He had a patch on his left elbow where he'd fallen on the cobblestones but said that a part from that he was fine. Ian asked him about Hector and Peter said that he had been knocked unconscious and taken to the hospital according to what he'd heard from other runners but that he was awake now and would do his best to make it to the Vodka party in the afternoon, another annual event hosted by the International Gutter Club.

"Well, that's a relief," said Ian.

"It is," said Frank. "I was worried about his head when I watched his fall on the TV."

"Nonsense, that man's got a cast iron skull. What worried me was that he might not make it to the Vodka party."

"Right," said Peter, smiling, "priorities."

"You know it," agreed Clive, "priorities."

"Well, in that case," said Peter, "there's another breakfast waiting for everyone on Calle San Agustín."

"True enough," said Ian, "time to go."

***

At the bar on Calle San Agustín the owner had set up four long tables on either side of the street with paper table cloths, silverware and plastic water glasses. With their group of five Frank counted twenty-five altogether. They were mostly local runners with a decent mix of foreigners. Everyone knew everyone except for Irina who was the only woman and who, as soon as she arrived, instantly became the new guest of honor. With her red hair, pale white skin and green eyes she was pretty and exotic and Spanish men were big fans of anything that hinted of faraway lands.

"*Huevos con txistorra* for everyone?" said Ian.

"No, I'll have the *tortilla española*," said Clive.

"Me too," said Irina who was sitting next to Clive.

"That's a potato tortilla," he told her.

"I know," she answered.

"OK, just wanted to make sure you knew."

"Thank you," she told him.

"And to drink?" asked Ian.

"How about a bottle of *vino tinto*, for starters?" said Peter.

"Good choice," said Frank.

The waitress brought out their wine bottle first along with the beers and the wine that the other twenty had ordered. They started drinking and talking and toasting and not too long afterwards their food arrived. They were all abundant portions and Irina was very hungry thinking that she hadn't had anything to eat since yesterday afternoon. She had, like many people who were partying in Pamplona, survived on a liquid diet of Vodka tonics and whatever else the men around her were offering.

The man sitting to Irina's left pointed to the bottle of red wine and asked her with his hands, much as a pantomime might have, if she wanted some.

"*Sí, gracias,*" she said, and he poured some into her plastic cup. She noticed that he was very tall and very thin and that his profile reminded her of Don Quixote with his tired eyes and aquiline nose, but without the beard. He had a yellow bandana on his head, which he never removed during the *fiesta*. He thought it went well with his

62

Atlético Madrid football jersey. It didn't and everyone told him that but he didn't care, he loved the team. Irina introduced herself and asked him what his name was and he pulled a pen out of his pocket and wrote it on his napkin, Checo.

"He can't speak," Clive explained, "but he can hear you and seems to understand a few words of English."

"OK," said Irina, and Checo tapped her on her shoulder and then pointed to himself and asked her with his hands in a sort of mute game of charades if she had seen him on TV today.

"No I haven't," she told him.

Checo moved his chair closer to her and using her left hand and both of his hands he gave her a visual diagram of what he had accomplished earlier during the first *encierro* of the *fiesta*. He showed her how with incredible agility and grace he had literally dashed between the horns of two of the six *toro bravos* that were running lead so that he could take the lead himself. He explained with his fingers that he counted seven seconds before he stepped out of their way and finished his run.

"Wow, that's something else," she said, "*muy bien*!"

Checo thanked her with his eyes and then took her hand again, raised it to his lips and kissed it.

Irina in turn gave him a kiss on the cheek and Clive told her that while it might not be obvious, Checo was very much a ladies man, a *caballero*, or at least he tried to be. He was also very poor but within this group of runners he felt himself a king and rightly so. He was the

63

best of the best and had been running since the 1970s and did things and succeeded where none of the others ever dared to go.

"Everyone takes care of him during the *fiesta*, buying him drinks and paying for his meals. I guess you could say that it's another tradition we have, one of the many," he told Irina.

"That's really sweet," she said, and it was then that she felt Clive's hand on her right knee.

"We do what we can," he told her.

"I'll bet you do," she said, thinking more about Clive doing whatever he wanted with her.

"Irina," said Frank, "after breakfast we can go back to my apartment if you want and get some rest before the Vodka Party."

"Sounds good," she told him, as Clive removed his hand.

Chapter 8

Frank held Irina's hand as they left the bar on Calle San Agustín. There were more people in the streets now and he didn't want to lose her. The *fiesta* was full of distractions and if he didn't keep his eye on her she could easily slip away. Something which he suspected she would do sooner or later anyway, with or without his permission, no matter how tightly he gripped her hand. There were *peña* bands, extra-large *papier mâché* puppets, or *gigantes* as the locals called them, jugglers, pick-pockets, children, *abuelitas* and everywhere you looked tired but generally happy people who were ready to start the new day with a clean slate and a game plan of the bars they would visit or the parties they would attend.

"¡*Cabrón!*" called a familiar voice behind them. Frank turned around and saw Eneko Ezkarra, a Basque artist friend of his who was about six foot two, had a beard that went down to his chest, crazy electric hair á la Albert Einstein and biceps that looked as thick as bull's neck.

"*Hombre, que pasa?*" said Frank, as Eneko embraced him in a bear hug and lifted him off his feet.

"What a surprise to see you, Ardito!"

"I got in yesterday."

"And you didn't call me, *cabrón. Y la chica es tuya?*" he asked.

"Almost mine," he told him in Spanish.

"What do you mean *casi?*"

"The affair hasn't been consecrated," Frank explained.

"*Coño!* What are you waiting for, Ardito?" said Eneko, laughing.

"You know how it is with the *fiesta.*"

"No, I don't, why haven't you done it yet?" he added, and then introduced himself to Irina.

"*Es un grande placer,*" he told her, "my name is Eneko and I am a friend of your *cabrón.*"

"Irina," she told him, "*placer mio.*"

"*Hablas castellano?*"

"A little."

"*Coño,* she's a keeper, Frank."

"You think so?"

"Absolutely, you are a very lucky *cabrón.* She is very beautiful and you are not," he said and laughed.

"Speak for yourself," said Frank, laughing.

"Let's go for a drink," Eneko suggested. "I know of a great bar around the corner."

"For you all the bars in this town are great."

"True, but this one is special, believe me."

Frank looked at Irina and told her that Eneko wanted to take them for a drink.

"That much I understood," she said.

"Well, what do you think? Drinks, or would you rather just go back to my place?"

"Let's get a drink."

"*Perfecto*," said Frank and soon they arrived at a small bar (for Pamplona standards) where Irina had her usual Vodka tonic and Frank and Eneko each ordered a pint of beer.

"Eneko's an artist," said Frank to Irina who looked up at the extra large Navarran.

"This is my work," he said, pointing to the print on his t-shirt. It was a picture of tiny stick people wearing red *pañuelos* and white clothing getting gored by bulls and falling off balconies on Calle Estafeta as they watched the *encierro*.

"Eneko is famous in Spain," Frank explained, "as a cartoon artist."

"I see," said Irina, who had spent most of her life in St. Petersburg and who had a pretty good idea of what art was but who wasn't sure if that included Eneko's stick people. She thought his t-shirt was funny and cute, but was it art? Maybe not, maybe yes. In the end, however, it wasn't a problem. She liked Eneko and that was the only thing that mattered.

"The t-shirts," said Frank, "that's his art, and his business."

"OK," she said.

"Frank, we need to talk about our book," said Eneko.

"*El Libro*?" said Frank.

"That's right, The Book. You haven't forgotten about our plans, have you?"

"No," Frank lied. When they had spoken about it last year during the *fiesta* they were both drunk and writing a book together seemed a wonderful idea, something that would facilitate Eneko's conquest of the US t-shirt market and at the same time raise from the dead Frank's floundering literary career. On that night of non-stop bar hopping Frank had spoken of their project as if it were a no-brainer, a kind of low hanging fruit with attached six-figure advance that was theirs for the taking. Eneko was going to do the illustrations and Frank would write the texts. The working title that they had come up with was "A Dream of the *Fiesta*", and in it he imagined himself as a kind of superhero who together with the local police helped solve violent crimes against both foreign tourists and locals. It was going to be a modern day "noir" but with *malas mujeres,* bulls and *patxaran* (the local liquor made from blackthorn berries). Of course, the next day when he woke up in time to run with the bulls he had forgotten pretty much everything of that conversation. Only now bits and pieces of it were coming back to him and he had to keep himself from laughing. These were the kinds of things you said when your brain was so thoroughly doused with alcohol that anything was possible. That was part of the fun of getting smashed, wasn't it? That you could act like an ass and no one ever took you seriously. So what was there that Eneko didn't understand about that night, he asked himself? He was never going to break into the US market and Frank's glorious future as a well-known and respected poet was dubious at best. If Eneko thought that an absolute nobody like Frank was going to save him from Spain's economic black hole then his situation was truly desperate.

Still, Eneko was a friend and Frank didn't want to hurt his feelings so, of course, he spoke about the book project in glowing terms and said that this time they would have to follow-up on their conversations and get the ball moving in the right direction. After finishing a second round the three of them left the bar and Eneko hurried off to meet another friend.

"We've got plenty of time before the Vodka Party," said Frank to Irina.

"Well, I don't really feel like resting."

"Sleep is way overrated," said Frank.

"Especially during the *fiesta*," added Irina and they both laughed.

He took her back towards the bullring where they stopped at the statue of Hemingway and left a half emptied bottle of *patxaran* that they had shared along the way as an offering to the town's real, albeit as yet unofficial, patron saint.

"They say that if you sprinkle a bit of *patxaran* on his beard and make a wish that Hemingway will make it come true," Frank told Irina.

"Really?" asked Irina.

"Probably not, but that's what I heard."

"I think it's possible," Irina told him. She looked down at their bottle, which was next to all the other bottles that had been offered before theirs, picked it up, poured some of the liquid into her hand and washed his beard with it.

"It has to be true," she said.

"That or this is where people leave their trash when the recycling bin starts to overflow," said Frank.

"Funny man."

"So what did you wish?" he asked her.

"You'll find out soon enough."

"No hints?"

"Nope," she told him and he took her hand and they continued their stroll around the Plaza de Toros looking at the numbered entrances in the *sol* or sunny side of the ring until they came to the massive metal doors in the rear of the Plaza, where the butchered carcasses of the bulls that would fight and die that afternoon would exit the ring in the refrigerated trucks of the province's many meat vendors.

"Have you ever been back here?" he asked her.

"No, this is my first year, remember?"

"True, I just thought that maybe you'd come down here yesterday."

"Didn't get that far."

"Sidetracked by an American?"

"*Sí, señor.*"

It was almost eleven and the sun was high in the cloudless blue sky and hot. They found some shade in a park that was built on a steep incline. It had a view of the river and there were grassy areas where people were having impromptu liquid picnics with bottles of sangria, *patxaran* and *Calimotxo*.

"How does this look?" Frank asked when he found a spot for the two of them.

"Good," said Irina.

"A little peace and quiet before we hit the Vodka Party," said Frank.

Irina sat down and had a look around and saw that there were many other couples there. Some looked as if they had passed out in each others arms and that they had been there since the night before sleeping the deep dreamless sleep of heavy drinkers. While another couple was very much awake and attempting what appeared to be a quiet copulation in the sunlight. No one paid them any heed because everyone was either too tired to look or unimpressed by the act itself.

"Where do you live?" Irina asked.

"Los Angeles."

"And what's it like in Los Angeles?"

"Dry and full of cars."

"And do you like it?"

"I was born and raised there. Can't really say if I like it or not. The weather's nice and you can surf or go for a swim at the beach if you don't mind the cold water."

"You're a professional surfer?"

"Right, I'm a champion."

"Really?"

"Not quite," he told her, "I paint houses."

"Seriously?"

"You don't believe me?"

"No, Frank Ardito does something more than just paint houses."

"He does?"

"He does," she said. "You're a gigolo."

"Funny," said Frank.

"Then you're a masseur."

"Bullseye," he said.

"I'm very intuitive."

"And if I had some rubbing oil, even corn oil would do, I'd have you strip down so that I could get to work on all your muscle groups."

"Should I go and see if anyone's carrying a bottle of olive oil?"

"You could."

"Or a stick of butter?"

"Can't say that I know of anyone who swears by it but I suppose that, in an emergency, we could use that, too."

"When push comes to shove."

"Exactly," said Frank. He didn't expect her to say that and it made him laugh. He liked her quick wit and her way with English expressions. She was a fast learner and unpredictable. In fact she had done nothing but surprise him since their first meeting at Café Iruña. Surprising was also the smoothness of her skin. He caught himself caressing her forearm from her wrist to her elbow and thinking that he had never felt skin as soft as that. Normally with these sensations with another woman there would be no containing him, but there was something about Irina that intimidated him, something else that caused him to hesitate.

"I think you know the kind of effect you have on men," he said.

"The what?"

"Nothing," Frank told her, "I was just thinking out loud."

"What time is it?" she asked.

"Around noon."

"I'm hungry," she said.

"Then let's find a bar," suggested Frank, who knew from past experience that it was never a good idea to hit the Vodka Party on an empty stomach.

Chapter 9

The Bodegón Sarria was more or less on the way to the Vodka Party. It wasn't exactly a straight line between two points but if Frank's objective was to nourish and gastronomically intrigue Irina then there was no better place to do it than at the Bodegón. The tavern had an ambiance that was both modern and rustic at the same time. There were the cured Serano ham legs hanging over the bar, the wooden rafters, the *pinchos* and the plates that you could order all on display. It was a very Spanish locale but more than that it was Navarran, which meant that it was some of the best that Spain had to offer in terms of food and drink.

Frank suggested that they keep it simple and get a plate of *Jamon Serano* for two with a basket of bread and two lagers.

"You're the expert here," said Irina.

The place was so packed that you couldn't see outside the windows. There were just people, people everywhere, standing next to you, waiting at the bar, sitting at the tables, standing around the tables. There was literally no room to move but the people moved just the same. It was full-on *fiesta* but no one was pushing. Everyone had to get somewhere but no one was going to get there fast and when they bumped into you they were polite about it and smiled and joked, apologized and wished you well.

"Here comes the food," said Frank. They had found a place up at the bar, miraculously enough, where there was standing room only. Frank paid the bartender and then he kissed Irina.

"To the two of us," he said, holding up his pint.

"To us," she said, looking at Frank and smiling.

"You think this place is packed enough?" he asked, before taking a sip from his beer.

"I'm sure they could still squeeze in some more if they wanted to."

"Under the tables, perhaps."

"Or in the toilets," she said and he laughed.

"God, it's good to be back here," said Frank.

"You missed it?" asked Irina, as she stuffed a piece of bread and ham into her mouth.

"Yes," he told her, as he picked up a piece of ham and took another sip from his beer. "I guess for someone like yourself who's here for the first time it's hard to understand, but yeah, I missed it."

"Well, I think I know how you feel. I know that I'll miss it too."

"To our melancholy days to come!" said Frank, raising his glass again.

"This ham is fantastic," said Irina.

"Everything here is good," Frank agreed and when they had finished the *jamon* and their pints they left the Bodegón, squeezing their way through the crowd until they were out and had been swallowed up into the sea of partygoers on Estafeta.

At the *curva* they took a right onto Calle de Curia and then left onto Calle del Carmen and then right again onto Calle de la Navarrería. From there it was straight up to the Cathedral and then left to the Caballo Blanco. The Vodka Party was just below the restaurant along the stone wall that was a part of the palisades of the *Casco Viejo*. There was a park there with a shaded gravel path. The International Gutter Club had set up their table of refreshments between two trees. The card-carrying members, aka owners, were easily recognizable with their extra large white dress shirts that had been embroidered with the club's name on the back and the name of the club member, in good standing, over the left hand pocket. Each member also had the flag of the country that they were from sewed onto the right sleeve of the club shirt just below the shoulder. Most of them were from Europe but there were a few Americans, some Canadians, Aussies and even a Cuban.

At the Gutter Club table there was a large punchbowl into which cartons of orange juice and bottles of Stolichnaya were poured. Below the table there were coolers filled with ice cubes. It was a hot day and the Gutter Club had promised in their leaflets that their party would be suitably chilled. As Irina and Frank approached the table, they were each carrying another drink that they had picked up in a bar on the way over from the Bodegón. Another British friend of Frank's, Dave, was at the punch bowl serving the drinks and when he saw Irina with a Cuba Libre in her hand he politely but firmly took it from her and dumped it unceremoniously into the trash bin behind him. He then gave her "a proper drink" and welcomed her to the party.

"Dave," he said to her, holding out his hand.

"Irina," she told him, smiling, as she took a sip from her new drink. "Oh, this is good."

"Strong enough? I can add some more vodka if you think it needs it."

"Perhaps a bit," she said, and Dave topped it off with a new bottle of Stolichnaya.

"How's that?"

"Much better," she said. "Thank you."

"Frank!" said Dave, as he handed him a drink. "I see life's been good to you this year."

"You mean Irina?"

"Bloody hell, where do you find 'em?"

"Here, at Café Iruña."

"You lucky s.o.b. Does she have a sister?"

"She has a brother if you're interested."

"If he's as pretty as his sister I might," said Dave who laughed and then told him that there was a cheese station set up against the wall.

"Don't tell me you're jealous?"

"*Claro*," said Dave, "who wouldn't be? Still don't understand how you do it."

"Good looks, women can't resist me," said Frank.

"More like charity, on her part," said Dave.

"Try love at first sight."

"You're making me laugh, Ardito."

"*Mi querido* Dave."

"Remember the cheese," Dave reminded him. "It's going fast and it won't last long."

"Will do," said Frank.

There were already a good number of people at the party. Frank could see Ian with a woman who looked new and Clive was there, but there was still no sign of Peter or Hector.

The cheese was a *queso de cabra ahumado,* a smoked goat cheese, and when he picked up a slice and put it in his mouth he immediately thanked the gods for Europeans in general and their traditions and in particular for Spain and this *fiesta.* The flavor was intense and subtle as it melted on his tongue. Why couldn't they make this in the USA, he asked himself. Of course, there were Americans who tried but it was never as good.

"Which is why I keep coming back," he said to himself, "one of the reasons, at least."

Frank piled some of the cheese on to a plastic plate and walked over to where Irina was standing with Clive and another couple.

"Hey Frank," said Clive.

"Hey Clive, have you tried this yet?" Frank asked, as he held out the plate of cheese.

"No, I haven't," said Clive.

"It's really good," said Frank.

"You're right," said Clive, as he ate a piece. Irina also took a slice, put it between her lips and brought it close to the woman who she was talking to so that she'd be able to bite it too. Her name was Marcy and she and her boyfriend were from Little Rock, Arkansas. It was their first time at the *fiesta* and she was wearing a pair of red hot pants, a white tank top and a stars and stripes American *pañuelo.* She was much taller than her boyfriend and reminded Frank physically of Jane Russell.

Her boyfriend was skinny and with a stern expression on his face. His nervous eyes betrayed the fact that he had yet to embrace one of the central tenants of the *fiesta,* namely that if you brought a woman to Pamplona there was nothing you could do to control her. You might think that you could but eventually when you had had enough to drink and had sufficiently internalized the *fiesta's* vibe you understood that any kind of control was a waste of time.

"Who's the woman with Ian?" said Frank to Clive.

"Her name is Debbie and she's actually an old flame."

"Come back to haunt him?" said Frank.

"Maybe."

"Where's she from?"

"New York City, I think."

"Any sign of Hector?" said Frank.

"Over there, look."

"Where?"

"By that group of Swedes," said Clive. Hector had a bandage on his forehead and his left arm was full of cuts and bruises from the fall.

"He seems to be enjoying himself. No worse for the wear and tear, I'd say," said Frank.

"He's a beast and he collects injuries like you collect girlfriends, Frank. He always has a new one to show off."

"And Peter?"

"No, haven't seen him," said Clive, who turned around to talk to Irina and Marcy only to discover that they were no longer there. He scanned the crowd and spotted them chatting with each other next to a tree at the edge of the party. Marcy's boyfriend, on the other hand, was still there and very drunk and he told Clive that he was going to the punch bowl.

"You want a refill?" he asked.

"Thanks," said Clive, handing him his plastic cup.

Frank kept an eye on Irina. Central tenants of the *fiesta* were all fine and well, but actually seeing his girlfriend seduce another woman was a surprise. He wasn't prepared for this, but then why should he be? This was the *fiesta de San Fermín*, right? Where anything goes, no? Still, it felt weird. Should he be jealous, curious or just indifferent? Irina was somewhere around her fourth vodka and orange juice and Marcy had had at least that many and certainly a few drinks before the party. They were taking selfies of each other together and with other people, telling jokes, saying silly things, flirting and laughing. They would walk arm in arm from one group to another, stopping to kiss the men or the women. They didn't seem to have any preferences. They stopped for a selfie with Ian and his date and kissed them both and then with Hector and the Swedes, then back to the punch table for another round. At the table Dave told Irina that he had an Ecstasy tablet for her to mix with her drink. It was mustard yellow and had a Chemise Lacoste alligator on one side and a happy face on the other.

"Do you think you can handle it?" said Dave.

"I'm Russian," she told him, smiling, "I'm pretty sure I can."

"Roger that," said Dave and he handed her the drug and her vodka. She looked at the tablet and then put it on her tongue and washed it down with the vodka. Marcy said that she wanted one too because they were sisters now.

"It's true we are," said Irina.

"Are you Russian?" said Dave to Marcy.

"No, but I am very athletic."

"How so?" Dave asked her.

"Stand over here for a second," she said, and Dave came out from behind the table and stood next to her.

"And now?" he asked.

"Now I want you to try to hit me anywhere."

"No, I can't do that," Dave told her with a smile.

"I want you to."

"OK, but I'm not really going to hit you."

"Alright, then pretend," she said, and Dave threw her a punch with his right arm which she easily avoided and then using his forward momentum she executed a maneuver that sent him flying onto the ground.

"What the fuck?" said Dave, as he recovered from the shock of the fall and looked up at Marcy and Irina from the gravel.

"I'm a black belt in Karate," said Marcy.

"Ah, right," said Dave, "that makes sense."

"Are you OK?" she asked. "I kinda exaggerated with the last part."

"You didn't mention the black belt."

"You wanted to see if I was athletic," she told him.

"And indeed you are, my dear," said Dave, as he got up from the ground and bushed the dirt off his trousers.

"So do I get a tablet?"

"Looks to me like you're ready for it," said Dave and he laughed, handing her the Ecstasy.

"Are you sure you're OK?" asked Marcy, who appeared seriously concerned.

"Nothing that a hot bath won't fix."

"You see what happens when you don't give the pretty women what they want," said Frank, walking over to the punch table for a refill.

"If you want, Ardito, I'm sure I could have a word with the young lady and see if she wouldn't mind repeating it but with you this time," said Dave.

"No, I think your fall was great, Dave, it's just that I didn't get it on video."

"What a shame," said Dave, taking Frank's cup and filling it up with more OJ and vodka.

"You going to the *corrida* today?" said Frank.

"I might, and you?"

"Don't have tickets."

"Ian's got tickets. He's always got tickets. Go see him, he'll set you up."

"Good idea."

"But I think you might need to get tickets for the three of you," said Dave, raising an eyebrow.

"The three of us?"

"You, Irina and Irina's new friend."

"The black belt?"

"They seem to have grown very fond of each other, don't you think?"

"You think so?"

"Of course, it might just be the tablets."

"Could be," said Frank.

"But, just in case, I'd get the black belt a ticket, too."

"And her boyfriend?"

"Isn't that him lying face down in the grass over there?"

"Light weight," said Frank.

"So, see, you don't have to worry about him. He's not going to be getting up for another couple of hours, at least."

"His loss," said Frank.

"And your gain," said Dave, as he continued pouring more refills.

"So long as she doesn't try that maneuver on me."

"Pretty soon, with all the booze and the tablet, she'll be lucky if she can hit the side of a building."

"True," said Frank.

"So have a chat with Ian. I'll make sure the girls don't elope without you knowing about it."

"OK," said Frank, "catch ya later."

He saw Ian standing near a stone bench set back in the grass against a wall that was a part of the Cathedral. His girlfriend had disappeared. He was talking with Clive and Hector and when he saw Frank he waved.

"Ardito, you wanker, your woman has abandoned you for another woman. Can't say that I blame her, but you might want to keep an eye on her."

"Ian, I need your help," said Frank.

"Too late for that now, Ardito."

"Seriously, Ian, I need some tickets for today's *corrida*."

"How many?"

"Three."

"I can do that if you don't mind sitting in the *parte sol*."

"How much are they?" said Frank.

"Twenty-five euros each."

"Seventy-five euros, are you serious?"

"Well, they're not nosebleed. They're about half way down."

"OK, here's seventy-five," said Frank. Ian handed Frank the three tickets and wished him the best of luck.

"Remember, tomorrow morning at the usual time at the flat on Estafeta if I don't see you before then," said Ian.

"Gotcha."

"*Y suerte!*" said Clive and both he and Ian started to laugh.

Chapter 10

Frank rounded up the girls and told them that he had tickets for the *corrida* and asked them if they wanted to go. Of course, they said. Neither of them had ever been but then they probably would have agreed to just about anything at that point. They were excited and Frank told them that they were in for a treat.

On their way out of the park Marcy almost tripped over her boyfriend as he lay snoring in the grass. She had completely forgotten about him.

At the corner of Mercaderes and Estafeta they joined the long procession of boisterous and noisy *peñas* that were making their way towards the bullring with their marching bands and satirical protest banners. There were about sixteen or seventeen *peñas* in Pamplona, the official ones at least, and each of them had a clubhouse in the *Casco Viejo* where they often organized dinners and other social events. Frank and the girls had fallen in with the *peña* Irrintzi whose members wore a distinctive black jacket similar to the ones that doctors wore in hospitals. Their band was playing a tune and everyone in the *peña* knew the words and was singing. They were also drinking and shouting and laughing and talking amongst themselves. The noise was incredible and Frank found it hard to understand what Irina and Marcy were saying to him. They had to scream into his ear and he had to do the same with them but they still couldn't hear him. It was chaos and everyone thought that that was just fine.

The Irrintzi members offered them wine and beer and whatever else that they were drinking. There were also others, usually men although not always, who were watching the *peña* parade and spraying water pistols filled with sangria at the *peñas* and in particular at the pretty women. Of course, it didn't take long for them to target Marcy and Irina because they were obviously foreign and quite attractive. Their white shirts quickly turned a shade of pink, as did their skin and their hair. Frank called them "cotton candy women" and they thought it was the funniest thing they had ever heard. They didn't mind at all. They were both drunk and happy and ready for anything that the *fiesta* could throw at them.

As they approached the end of Estafeta where the street started to open up, Frank was asked by some of the Irrintzi members if he and the girls wanted to join them for the *corrida*. Frank said that he already had three tickets and he doubted if they would be anywhere near where Irrintzi had their block of seats. The heaviest of the three men from Irrintzi, who was now his friend, or drinking buddy at least, had a look at his tickets and said that, yes, they were not close to Irrintzi, that they were closer to Anaitasuna, another *peña*, but that it didn't matter, Frank and the girls could go with them.

"Even with these tickets?" said Frank.

"That doesn't matter when you're with the *peña*," said Nacho, the heavy one and leader of the group, "we can get you in."

"*Fantastico*," said Frank. "*Muchisímas gracias*."

"*Hombre, de nada*." Don't mention it, said Nacho.

"What's going on?" asked Irina.

86

"We're going to stay with this group," Frank told her, and Irina filled Marcy in on their new plans. Marcy jumped up and down to show how excited she was, her ample breasts bouncing riotously up and down with her. Marcy's pupils were so dilated that Frank was sure that with all the alcohol and the tablet of Ecstasy she would have been just as excited to hear that they were going to throw her into the ring with the fighting bulls.

The Irrintzi seats were in the *sol* part of the ring but closer to the *sol y sombra* section than the ones that Ian had sold him. They were also in a *tendido bajo* rather then in a *tendido alto*, which meant that they were closer to the ring itself and had a better view of the *corrida*. Being in the *sol* section meant that during the *corrida* the sun would always be shining on them and the sun in July in Pamplona during the day was something that you did not want to endure without liquids. For this reason the bullring was full of bars where you could buy beer and water and other drinks and stay hydrated. Bringing your own alcohol in from outside, however, was strictly prohibited and yet that was never a problem for the *peñas*. They carried in huge coolers full of alcohol right by the guards who were checking everyone's bags and no one ever said anything. Obviously being a local had its advantages.

On hot days people wore straw hats, village people hats, leather biker hats, white hats, green hats, pink hats, and anything else that the North African street vendors were selling to keep the sun off their heads. They also fanned themselves with *albanicos* (the traditional Spanish fan) and the *corrida* programs.

There were essentially two worlds and two different kinds of people who came to see the bullfights. In the shaded areas, the *sombra* seats, especially those in the *barrera* or *contrabarrera*, right next to the ring, sat the well to do. They had generally paid a good deal of money for their seats and loved the *fiesta* and *corrida* and everything that had to do with it. They were true *aficionados* and the way they behaved was similar to the way people behaved in any other bullring in Spain, with the exception of Pamplona during the *fiesta*. They did not shout or throw food or drink at each other and while like everyone else they dressed in the traditional red and white their clothes were usually spotless and pressed. More often than not they were also politically conservative and back in the days of the Franco regime these people supported the power of the Spanish government in Pamplona.

The *sol* seats were and still are the cheap seats. They were also the refuge and playground of those who detested the fascist regime. All of the *peñas* sat in the *sol* sections and during the fascist years they protested and partied during the bullfights and they still do that today. Bullfighting, which is also referred to as *la fiesta nacional*, was heavily promoted and subsidized by the Franco dictatorship and to this day there are many in the *peñas* who refuse to watch the *corrida*. They literally stand up and turn their backs to the bullring. It's a form of protest and a message to the *aficionados* and powerful in the shaded seats that for them being with their friends and partying will always be more important than *la fiesta nacional*.

Frank had been to bullfights before and had a reasonably good idea of what was going on and how Spain in the past had seen itself mirrored in *corrida* and how even today bullfighting remained deeply embedded in the Spanish psyche. But for Irina and Marcy everything before them was new and strange and they had many questions for Frank.

"Why is everyone wearing these black jackets?" asked Irina

"You'll see soon enough," Frank told her.

"It's a secret?" said Marcy.

"Better than that, it's a surprise," said Frank.

"Oh, I love surprises," said Irina.

"Ladies," said Frank, "the show is about to begin."

The large gates at the rear of the Plaza were opened and two men wearing black capes and feathered black tricorne hats from the eighteenth century entered the ring on *pura raza española* horses and rode to the other side where they stopped and tipped their hats to the president of the jury. They then separated and galloped back one to the left side of the ring and the other to the right to the rear gates where they waited for the three matadors who would be fighting that day. The matadors walked into the ring dressed in their traditional *traje de luces*, or suit of lights, with their left arms wrapped in a ceremonial cape, the *capote de paseo*. Then came their retinue, or *cuadrilla*, of *banderilleros* and the *picadores* on their armored and blindfolded horses. After them the workers who kept the ring clean and who hauled away the carcasses of the bulls after they had been killed. All of them following the two men with the feathered black tricorne hats walked across the ring to the other side and saluted the president of the jury.

"What's happening now?" said Marcy, who was holding Irina's hand.

"It's the *paseíllo*. They're paying their respects to the president of the jury."

"A jury? Who's being judged?" asked Marcy.

"The matadors will be," said Frank.

"On what?" asked Irina.

"Basically on whatever art these guys create today."

"Art?" said Irina. "What does art have to do with this?"

"Everything and nothing, I guess," said Frank, smiling.

"You couldn't be a bit more vague?" joked Marcy.

"Well, those who follow bullfighting, the *aficionados*, say that this isn't a contest between the bull and the bullfighter to see who wins. Sport and the idea of winning or losing have nothing to do with *corrida* and this is what most Americans don't understand when they say: "Oh, I hope that the bull finally wins." The bull is never going to win."

"Never?" said Marcy.

"Never," repeated Frank, "because even in the worst case scenario where the bull actually kills a matador the bull itself will still have to be killed. The senior matador or the next senior matador, if the senior matador is killed, will have to kill the bull, by law."

"Well, that doesn't seem very fair," said Irina, who gave Frank a kiss on the cheek.

"As I said, there's no winning here for the bull. He was raised for this, born and bred for the arena, so to speak."

"OK, we get that, but this art business, where does that come in?" said Irina.

"You'll see," he told her.

The three *toreros* exchanged their *capotes de paseo* for the large capes, the *capotes de brega,* the ones that were yellow on one side and pink on the other and that they would use when the bulls entered the ring. All the men on horseback along with the clean up crews exited the ring. The *banderilleros* stayed with the bullfighters behind the wooden barriers.

The sun was very hot and the *peña* bands were all playing different tunes at the same time when the first matador walked to the center of the ring with his *capote.* He took off his hat and left it in the sand, to which the crowd roared and the *peña* bands played even louder.

"Why is everyone cheering?" said Irina.

"Because he's dedicated his first bull to everyone here," said Frank.

"Of course, it's obvious, why didn't I think of that?" said Irina.

The matador, who was tall and thin and who looked to be in his late twenties, walked towards the gate where the bull would make its entrance. On the screens Frank saw the bull's name, Universo, its color, light brown and its weight, six hundred kilos. When the matador was about seven or eight meters from the gate he stopped and went down on his knees holding the heavy, pressed cotton cape in front of him.

"What's he doing?" said Marcy.

"They're going to let the bull out of that gate," Frank told her.

"And he's decided to greet him on his knees, isn't that kind of insane?" said Irina.

"Somewhat," agreed Frank, who saw it as more of a circus stunt than the best of what the art of bullfighting had to offer.

"Hope he doesn't get hurt," said Marcy.

"He's made the sign of the cross. That should help," said Frank with a smile.

"Better than nothing," said Marcy.

The matador was shaking his cape, lifting it up and spreading it evenly over the ground in front of him, preparing himself for the moment when Universo would come charging out of the gate.

"Watch the cape," said Frank to Irina.

The gate opened and the bull was a flash of power and fury as he surged into the arena. His horns were down and in the position that would allow him to toss the matador easily into the air. But about two meters before the bull reached his target the *torero* gracefully swirled the *capote de brega* over his left shoulder and the animal instead of hitting the matador followed the cape.

"Well, I'd say he's earned his pay today just with that one move," said Frank, as the *peña* bands, theirs included, started to play again, each with its own song.

"And that's it?" said Marcy.

"That's just the beginning, now comes the real bullfighting."

As the matador continued to lead the bull in a series of passes to test its speed and whether it preferred the left or the right, the Irrintzi members were handing out plastic cups filled with *sidra,* which was a popular drink in Pamplona during the *fiesta* and that was usually served chilled from a bottle held at arms length above one's head and poured so that the arc of the falling cider would land more or less directly into the glass or plastic cup that you wanted to fill. It was something that required a certain amount of skill and those who had a talent for pouring cider did tricks such as pouring it over their shoulder with one hand and catching it behind their back with the other.

"*Quieres?*" asked Nacho, holding a plastic cup out to Irina.

"He's asking you if you want some. It's cider, try it," said Frank.

"How do you say sure?"

"*Por supuesto,*" said Frank.

"*Por supuesto,*" repeated Irina who took the glass full of cider.

"And your *amiga?*" asked Nacho.

"Oh sure, I'll try it," said Marcy.

"*Muy bien,*" said Nacho.

The matador had by then finished checking out the bull and he retreated behind the barrier. It was now time for the first act of the *corrida,* the *tercio de varas.* The matador's two *picadores* entered the arena on their armored mounts. Each of them carrying a long lance called a *vara.*

"Who are these guys?" said Marcy.

"They're *picadores,*" said Frank.

"They look mean and pretty at the same time. Are they the matador's hit men?"

"No," said Frank.

93

"And they're not there to protect him?"

"Not even."

"So what's their deal?" asked Marcy.

"They prepare the bull for the fight."

"How?"

"Watch," said Frank.

The first of the two *picadores* approached the bull, which was standing in the shaded side of the arena. The *picador* positioned himself and his horse between the bull and the barrier. The bull looked at him calmly but did nothing until the *picador* shouted at the bull. At that point the bull charged and as it hit the padded, blindfolded horse the *picador* thrust his lance deep into the bull's *morillo*, the large neck muscle just behind its head. The bull was not deterred and pushed even harder against the horse and its master. The *picador* responded with a second even deeper thrust. The crowd then started to whistle and shout their disapproval saying that enough was enough, *ya basta!*, that the *picador* was destroying the bull. But the *picador* ignored the crowd. He worked for the matador and it was the matador who told him how he wanted the bull and how many times the bull would have to be lanced.

"When is he going to stop?" said Irina.

"When the bull is ready," said Frank.

"This is so cruel," said Marcy. "Why is he doing this?"

"Because he can't fight the bull unless he reduces its mobility. Did you see how agile the bull was when he first entered the ring? A matador can never fight a bull like that. Certainly not up close."

"But that's not fair!" said Marcy.

"*Mi querida* Marcy, remember, this has nothing to do with being fair. It's just the way they do things here."

"For art?" said Irina.

"For art," said Frank.

When the *picador* was satisfied with his work he rode away from the bull and exited the ring with the other *picador*. Now it was time for the second act. A *banderillero* carrying two *banderillas*, which were basically wooden shafts each with a single metal barb, entered the arena and stood at a distance from the bull. When he was ready he jumped up to get the bull's attention. The bull charged and the *banderillero* holding both of the "little flags" in his right hand side stepped to the left of the bull and placed the *banderillas* into its *morillo* with an elegant arching maneuver. The crowd approved and there were shouts of *Olé* and in the sunny side of the ring one of the *peña* bands played their version of Queen's "Another one bites the dust."

"Why is he putting those things in the bull?" asked Irina.

"I've heard that maybe it's to correct the bull's natural tendency to favor one side over the other, but I'm not sure about that. It's something you could ask Clive next time you see him."

"Oh, there's another one with the…what are they called?"

"*Banderillas.*"

"Yeah, those thingies."

This time the *banderillero* ran at the bull and tried to place both of the *banderillas* going over its horns but one of them missed and fell to the ground. The bull now had three *banderillas* hanging from the left side of his neck muscle and they moved whenever he moved.

95

"That one wasn't very good," said Marcy.

"No one's perfect," said Frank.

"Hey, do you think you could ask Nacho for some more of this? It's kinda hot out here."

"Sure," said Frank and he handed Marcy's cup to Nacho who was just then throwing ice-cubes in the direction of another *peña*.

"*Un momento*," said Nacho, as he dried his hands on his trousers. He was tall and looked like someone who lifted weights.

"Thanks," said Frank when Nacho handed him another *sidra*.

"*De nada*."

Frank handed the plastic cup to Irina who passed it on to Marcy. The last *banderillero* didn't miss and the bull now had five metal barbs embedded in its *morillo*. "So, have they finished with their sado-maso art installation?" asked Marcy, who was laughing and blowing kisses to the bull.

"Now comes the finale," said Frank.

"The last act," said Irina.

"Exactly."

From where they were they could see the matador speaking with someone from his *cuadrilla*. It was his *mozo de espada*, the man in charge of his swords. He handed the *torero* the cape and the first sword that he would use in his *faena*. The bull was standing in the center of the ring and stomped its hoof into the sand. The gold embroidery on the matador's red *traje de luces* glittered in the sunlight. He began to walk slowly towards the bull. He could hear the chaotic noise of the many *peña* bands and watched the men and women who were dancing in the *tendidos* with their plastic cups and bottles and smiled when he thought that he had finally made it to Pamplona on the day of its patron saint. He could feel such energy here and vowed that he would give them something to remember him by.

"Who makes the first move, the bull or the man?" said Irina.

"Usually the matador. He'll try to get the bull's attention with his *muleta*."

"What's a *muleta*?"

"The small cape that he's using."

"He's moving his cape now, but the bull isn't buying it."

"It's standing its ground," said Frank, "but watch. Notice how he stretches his left leg forward keeping the cape just behind his hip, inching his way towards the bull."

"Yet the bull refuses to move," said Irina.

"He'll move," Frank assured her.

When the bull decided that the matador had gone far enough it took the *torero*'s bait and charged. The matador began the dance between the two with a series of five *naturales* and then another series of *derechazos*. It was a brilliant performance and even those who knew nothing of *corrida* were impressed by the elegance and the sensuality of his moves. With every pass he kept bringing the bull closer, risking everything, dangerously exposing himself to the bull's horns that passed mere millimeters from his skin. It was one of those rare moments when the matador and the bull were worthy of one another. Many in the Plaza were on their feet and cheering him on, even in the more sedate *tendidos*. The matador was close to the end of his *faena* and had positioned himself so that the bull following his cape would pass directly behind his shoulders in a move that was called a *predresiana*. Instead the bull gored him in the thigh just below his hips and flipped him head over heals into the air. It was so fast that before anyone could even realize what had happened the bull had spun around and was ready to finish him off hitting him again with its horns in the matador's abdomen and his right arm.

"That's not good," said Irina, putting her hand over her mouth.

"Not good at all," agreed Frank, who looked over in Marcy's direction and saw that finally she had nothing to say.

Immediately the *banderilleros* entered the arena and distracted the bull with their large capes. The matador was then picked up by four other men and carried outside to an ambulance that was waiting to take him to the hospital.

"So this time the bull wins, right?" asked Marcy.

"The bull must die," Frank told her.

"Even if he wins?"

"It's the law," said Frank.

"What law? Why can't they just declare the bull the winner and call it a day?" said Marcy, whose cheeks were red from all the alcohol and who stood there smiling, with her pretty legs and slender waist, almost as if she were challenging him to tell her that she was wrong.

"Remember what I said about the senior matador taking over?"

"Sort of."

"Well, there he is."

"The matador? He's not coming back," said Marcy.

98

"I know that."

'So who is this guy?"

"The one who is going to kill the bull."

"Not fair."

"You're right," said Frank, letting her have the point.

The senior matador finished the job on his first try. It was a quick and clean kill with the bull dropping to its knees almost immediately. The clean up crew came out with their two horses, hooked the bull's horns to the harness and pulled it out of the arena to the *abattoir* in the rear where the animal would be butchered and its meat sold in the local markets.

After that there were other bulls and other kills with plenty of drinking and eating, dancing and music and then it was over. The *peñas* hopped over the barriers into the arena and walked out the front doors of the bullring, *en masse*, in a long, noisy and very inebriated procession that finished in Plaza Castillo.

Frank and the girls were still with Irrintzi and Nacho said that if they didn't have anything better to do they could join them for a bit of bar hopping.

"What did he say?" asked Irina.

"He says they're going to drink some more and then eat some more and then perhaps drink some more after that. Should we stay with them?" asked Frank.

"You're the boss!" said Irina, and Marcy took her hand and twirled her and they both tripped and fell on top of each other laughing.

Chapter 11

It was standing room only at Chez Belagua, a *sidreria*/café that the members of Irrintzi had adopted as one of their official meeting places. The café that night was so packed that most of the people drinking there were standing outside on Calle Estafeta. In addition to cider they also served beer and pretty much any kind of cocktail that you could think of. Irina and Marcy had returned to their vodka mixes while Frank and Nacho stayed with beers for the time being.

Frank felt good and thought that in spite of the fact that he'd been drinking since noon he wasn't drunk. He'd been going up and down the alcohol gradient with vodka and cider and now the beers and in theory that was supposed to get you seriously sloshed. Yet, he could touch his nose with his finger the way you were supposed to, bringing it in slowly without stopping from arm's length. He did it twice and succeeded both times.

"What are you doing?" asked Irina.

"I'm checking to see if I am sober," he told her.

"You look sober to me," said Nacho.

"How can you tell?" asked Marcy.

"Easy," he said. "Frank, close your eyes and touch Marcy's nose."

"OK, but she can't blame me if I end up poking her in the eye."

"Don't worry," said Nacho, and Frank closed his eyes.

"Now, Frank, I'm going to turn you around three times, slowly," said Nacho.

"You are so not going to pass this test," said Irina, as she watched Frank start to spin.

"OK, that's one turn, starting the second," said Frank.

"How do you feel?" said Nacho.

"Fine. How am I supposed to feel?"

"Soon you'll feel much better," Nacho promised, and just as Frank started his third turn Nacho gave him a strong shove that sent him flying into Marcy. Frank instinctively put his arms out in front of him to brace for the fall and ended up grabbing both of Marcy's breasts. When he realized what had happened everyone was laughing.

"*Hombre*," said Nacho. "There are only two possibilities here. One, that you are very drunk, or two, that you are feeling much better now."

"Can't argue with that," said Frank who looked at Marcy and saw that she wasn't at all upset and that if anything she liked it.

"To Frank's ultra rapid reflexes," said Irina, raising her Vodka tonic.

"To his reflexes," they toasted above the noise of the bar and the street.

"I think soon we're going to be leaving for another locale where we can dance. Do you want to come?" said Nacho to Frank.

"You ladies feel like dancing?" Frank asked.

"Why not?" said Irina.

"Yeah, let's go," said Marcy, and the four of them along with a few others from Irrintzi set out in the direction of the bullring.

"It's not very far from here," said Nacho to Irina.

101

"Oh, I'm fine. I could walk all night."

"Well, that's good because there are many places that I'd like to show you in Pamplona."

"And Frank and Marcy, too," she reminded him.

"Of course," said Nacho.

The bar with an open-air discotheque was on Calle de Juan de Labrit. It was right across the street from the bullring and from what Frank could see the crowd was mostly twenty and thirty somethings with a smattering of forty year olds thrown in for good measure. They had a DJ and he was playing all the summer hits plus his own collection of Spanish rock and dance music from the seventies on up. Colored lights moved across the floor of the disco and were synched with the music.

More drinks were bought with the ladies sticking with their Vodka tonics while Frank ordered a Rum Collins. Nacho had another beer.

"This is an alcoholic's wet dream," said Frank, "the bartenders are more than competent, they can make whatever you want and it's incredibly cheap."

"The recession has lowered the prices, but the know-how and the service have always been good in Pamplona. We pride ourselves on that," said Nacho.

"You know, I look at those two and I'm reminded of the Jonathan Richman song, *I was dancing at the lesbian bar*."

"Lesbians? You think so?" said Nacho, looking alternatively pensive and amused, as he watched Irina and Marcy improvise a tango/fondling session on the dance floor.

"Well, no, not really. I don't think Irina is, at least. Perhaps the American is, but I doubt it."

"Here in Spain you see women together all the time and no one thinks anything of it."

"Yours is a civilized country," said Frank.

"In some ways it is, and then in other ways it isn't at all."

"Right, the bullfighting, for instance."

"Among other things," said Nacho.

"It's very traditional," said Frank.

"It is and it isn't," Nacho explained.

"Sort of like the United States."

"No, over there your home-grown Jacobins are ruling the roost, on the right and the left, there's little difference. No offense, but you are and always have been a nation of radical puritans."

"No offense taken, but you really think so? Even with all the identity politics?"

"*Hombre,* America is America and you can't change that. Every country has its own personality or DNA and in the States they like to psychologically micro-manage you. People are constantly being told what they should think, what words they should use, or not use, even what they should believe, and that kind of intolerance smacks of radical puritanism to me. There's no freedom in the USA and everything a man does or even just thinks of doing has become a potential crime," said Nacho, as he finished his beer.

"I have to agree with you."

"*Es mejor aqui en España,*" he said.

"Much better," agreed Frank.

"So why are you over there? You're Spanish is good. You would have no problem in Spain."

"I don't know, but you're right. Perhaps I should start thinking about it."

"There's no rush, we'll be waiting for you when you do decide. In the meantime it's *fiesta* and the night is young," said Nacho.

"We should join them, don't you think?" said Frank, looking at Irina and Marcy.

"Can I have the Russian?" asked Nacho.

"No, you can take the American."

"Let's flip for her," said Nacho, taking a euro coin out of his pocket, "heads I win, tails she's yours."

"Fair enough," said Frank, and Nacho flipped the coin and it was tails.

"Looks like she stays with me," said Frank, and they laughed and drank to the inevitable victory of freethinking men and women everywhere.

"Watch out," said Frank, "here comes trouble."

"Where?"

"See that guy there?"

"The short skinny one?" said Nacho.

"Yeah, him."

"The one who looks like he's been sleeping in the grass?"

"That's Marcy's boyfriend," said Frank.

"He doesn't look too happy."

"He should be," said Frank, "we kept his woman out of trouble, took her to the *corrida*, plastered as she was."

"I doubt he appreciates the favor," said Nacho, smiling.

"Should we intervene?"

"No," said Nacho, "let him handle it."

Perhaps he was as drunk as she was, thought Frank, but it didn't take long for them to make up. At first her boyfriend looked angry but then Marcy said something into his ear and he visibly relaxed. He took her hand, they kissed and then they left the bar without saying good-bye to anyone.

"Well, that was quick," said Frank.

"Easy come, easy go," said Nacho, as Irina joined them at their table.

They stayed there for a while, talking and dancing and drinking, but by eleven they had left to find another bar that Nacho wanted them to see. It was at the other end of the old town and the streets were still packed. Frank held Irina's hand tightly so that he wouldn't lose her in the crowd, but by then she was so drunk that she wanted to run away from him. To no place in particular, any place would do where Frank couldn't reach her.

"Let me go!" she said, and before he knew it she had freed herself from his grip and had started off down another street with

105

Nacho. They weren't moving too fast because of the crowd and Nacho was easy to spot. He looked like an NBA basketball center compared to everyone else.

At first he thought, to hell with it, let her go, but then he changed his mind and followed them at a distance. He had never thought of himself as a stalker, but then again, why not? He didn't have anything better to do, and she was, theoretically at least, still his girlfriend. They walked down Calle de Javier and when they got to the Kaos Bar they stopped for more drinks. Frank waited on the other side of the street and as Nacho and Irina squeezed through the entrance Nacho's hand was cupping her ass. On their way out they were holding plastic cups that looked like OJ and vodka. Irina liked to drink and Nacho, no doubt, was doing his best to keep her happy. They moved along slowly, taking their time as they weaved in and out of the crowd and stopping to kiss as they came to the intersection with Calle Dormitaleria. There they turned left and headed in the direction of the Cathedral with Frank secretly following them. He had an idea where they were going and sure enough after they had passed the Cathedral they continued up the alley and around the Caballo Blanco to the gravel road that led them to the site of the Vodka Party.

There was hardly anyone there, just a few shadows in the distance. Frank watched them from the wall as they stood together in the grass holding each other. Perhaps if either of them had bothered to look they might have noticed him but they were too busy kissing and unzipping and moving whatever needed to be moved. Nacho lifted her jean skirt up to her waist and then held her as she removed her slip. He then went down on his knees and buried his tongue between her legs, wrapping his arms around her and feeling the beauty of her body with his fingers. She moaned as he held her tight and after she had come the first time and he thought that she was ready he lifted her up from the ground and carried her all the way to the monastery wall, where he made her scream with pleasure, as he pushed into her as deeply as he could go.

Frank watched it all, mute and pale, and when in the end they both collapsed into the grass exhausted he had seen enough and walked away.

Chapter 12

When Frank got up the next morning for the run he could still see Irina's stuff lying around the living room. He figured that eventually she would be coming back to collect what was hers but he wasn't at all sure after what he'd seen last night if she would ever be sleeping there again. The *fiesta*, in fact, could affect people in strange ways. There was no doubt about it. It acted as a kind of catalyst releasing energies that often times you never knew existed. As such he wasn't surprised by Irina's behavior, a woman could change radically in seconds and then flip back after a couple of hours to the way she'd been and no one ever gave it a second thought. It was just the *fiesta* and the atmosphere here that everyone breathed.

Yet, even if the probabilities were high that he would never get the chance to go to bed with her Frank was sure of one thing, Irina would not be running today. She had run yesterday with very little sleep but doing it again after a night of carousing and the outdoor performance with Nacho was highly unlikely. Frank himself was running on fumes, but he was used to it and what's more he needed it. Running with the bulls for Frank, as it was for Ian and the others, gave meaning to his life. In a sense it defined him and when he ran he was focused as he hardly ever was outside of the *encierro*. Indeed, Frank thought that if Hector could have his Paleolithic visions of stampeding Aurochs then why shouldn't he be entitled to a few Zen-like moments of clarity whenever he was running?

Turning onto Estafeta Frank saw Hector standing on the other side of the street absolutely still and looking in his direction as if he'd just seen a ghost.

"Hector," he shouted. "You OK?"

"Yeah man," he said, smiling his big toothy grin. "I just had a vision."

"Come on," said Frank, "I'm sure we can find some coffee for you up in the apartment."

"No, really, Frank. I was looking at a shaman, a man of knowledge."

"And what did he tell you?"

"He said that I was out of balance and that being bipolar was my natural state and that I should stop taking the pills."

"You mean your medication?"

"Yeah, the lithium. He said that it blocked the energy flow that I needed to reach the other worlds."

"Other worlds?" said Frank with a grin.

"Different planes of perception, as real as the one we're in."

"Sounds like I better get you up to Ian's for that coffee, pronto."

"I swear I saw him, Frank," said Hector, taking hold of his friend by the arm.

"No doubt you did," said Frank, "but I still think you need a coffee."

***

On the sixth floor Ian was looking at the photos from yesterday's *encierro* in the Diario de Navarra and commenting on the various knock-downs and near misses.

"Bloody hell, did you guys see this one of Hector?"

"Which one," asked Clive, "before, after or during?"

"Didn't know that there were so many," said Peter, wearing his usual black shirt, which he would wear for the duration of the *fiesta*.

"This one," said Ian, "where he gets hit by the bull."

"The bull didn't hit him. He got pushed from behind," said Peter.

"Hit or pushed from behind whatever happened he was knocked out," said Clive.

"What time is it?" asked Ian.

"Seven thirty-five," said Peter.

"Where are they?"

"Who?" asked Clive.

"Hector and Frank, that's who," said Ian.

"I wouldn't be surprised if Frank was still doing it with his Russian cutie," said Clive.

"I sure as hell wouldn't be here," said Ian.

"Me neither," said Peter.

"I wouldn't kick her out of my bed, that's for damn sure," said Clive, and it was then that they heard the intercom.

"Can one of you get that? It might be Don Giovanni," said Ian.

"I'll go," said Peter, who walked to the door and pressed the button. "Hello," he said.

"It's us," said Frank, and Peter opened the downstairs door.

"So?" said Ian.

"Don Giovanni and his consort," said Peter.

"The leggy Russian?"

"No, the berserker boxer friend."

"Send him back," said Ian, "I want the Russian."

"Too late," said Clive, as the doorbell rang, "they're here."

"What took you so long?" Ian asked.

"Foot traffic," said Frank.

"More like one last shag for the road," said Ian.

"Well, we're here, where's the coffee?"

"Over in the kitchen," said Clive, and Frank poured a cup for himself and for Hector.

"Here," said Frank, handing Hector his cup, "this will clear your thoughts."

"Thanks."

"So whose bulls are they running today?" asked Peter.

"Jandilla," Ian told him.

"Could be worse," said Clive, "could have been Cebada Gago."

"They're up tomorrow," said Ian.

"As if Cebada bulls would be worse than any other ranch. Breeding isn't the thing. What counts is the moment, the morning they run, the weather, the number of people running with them and god only knows what else. Every day is different," said Peter.

"And on any day anything can happen," said Hector.

"Exactly," said Peter.

"I still think that Cebada, genetically, is more of a bad-ass bull," said Clive.

"Bullshit," said Ian, and Peter laughed.

"It only appears that way because Cebada has run in more *encierros*, thirty as opposed to Jandilla's nineteen," said Peter.

"And the more times they run the easier it is to nail wankers like Hector in the ass," added Ian.

"Ha, ha," said Clive, "but seriously for a second, we've all been doing this for a while. Tell me that there isn't a difference between Jandilla or Cebada Gago and Miura bulls for example."

"Miura bulls are huge," said Frank.

"But…" said Clive.

"But they tend to stick together and that's why they run them when they know they're going to have a lot of people out there. The herd stays together, less gorings," said Frank.

"Whereas Cebada bulls are like 500 kilo Tasmanian Devils, sowing destruction and chaos wherever they go," said Clive.

"They're not friendly," said Hector.

"And I wouldn't recommend them as pets," said Peter, "but genetically more predisposed to rampage, that I doubt."

"Genetics is everything," Clive reminded everyone.

"Hey guys, I hate to break up our discussion but it's time for us to go, they've opened the barrier and the runners are moving up Estafeta."

"*Vamonós*," said Hector, and they filed out the door and down the six flights to the entrance hall. Ian said *suerte* to the others and asked Frank if he wanted to run on Santo Domingo instead of Estafeta.

"Sure," he told him, "why not?" It was the first part of the run and most of it was walled off on both sides and so there was no place to hide when the bulls came charging up from the pens.

"As the Sioux chief said to Dustin Hoffman in Little Big Man, today is a good day to die."

"Don't worry, Ian isn't gonna let you die today."

"Much obliged," said Frank, as they walked back towards the City Hall and then down Santo Domingo, where they stopped at the runner's shrine to San Fermin. The small figure that was no more than a foot and a half tall sat in a stone cubicle along with a few candles that were usually lit. To the right and to the left and directly below the Saint were the *pañuelos* of all the *peñas*. A few minutes before the bulls were let out the runners stood in front of the shrine and recited in Spanish and then in Basque a little speech that asked the Saint to protect them during the *encierro* and to give them his blessing.

Whether it worked or not was anyone's guess, but after you had run the *encierro* a few times you began to understand that more often than not luck was the only thing that stood between you having a very good run and a disastrous one. So for this reason it was better to ask San Fermin for his blessing. Maybe it was all a hoax, another Christian-Judaic fairytale, but if it wasn't, and you hadn't asked for his protection? Then you were screwed.

113

"I read somewhere that 69% of the gorings happen here on Santo Domingo," said Frank to Ian.

"I don't believe in statistics," said Ian, "tell me what the odds are and then I'll listen."

"The odds?"

"The chances of either one of us getting pricked by a bull while we're surrounded by all these other guys," said Ian.

"I don't know."

"Pretty fucking small, that's what."

"But Hector was gored."

"And so what? Hector wanted to get pricked. He thinks it'll make him into a warrior like Peter."

"Apparently."

"Whereas you and I we're smart," said Ian. "We don't stick our arses in front of a bull and say come and get it."

"Damn right," said Frank.

"We get close, sure, but we don't risk it, 'cause we're not daft. We need our arses, and what's more, we love life."

"Amen to that," said Frank.

"It's about time," said Ian, looking at his watch. From where they were standing they could see the pen and they would have a good view of the rockets going up and the gates as they swung open.

"*Suerte*," said Frank to Ian and to two other men who were standing next to them.

"*Suerte* to you too, Ardito," said Ian, as the first of the two rockets was lit. It made a loud swish and then a bang as it exploded in

114

the blue sky above them. The gates were opened, the bulls scrambled out of their holding pen and both Frank and Ian started to run.

The herd was compact with three of the six *toro bravos* taking the lead. They were running up the right side of Santo Domingo, as they often did, which is why Frank and Ian ran on the left. Frank was ahead of Ian and he could see the bulls coming up fast behind them. The lead bull on the right of the triad was already tossing runners into the air like they were bowling pins as it cleared space against the wall. All this while he kept pace with the other two bulls, never slowing down.

Frank had seen them do this before in other runs but their speed, agility and sheer power never ceased to impress him. He respected the bulls and feared them but he knew that it was also a privilege to run with these animals, to sense their strength and fearlessness on this last morning of their lives.

Now as to whether it was right or wrong to continue having *encierros* Frank didn't think that it was a question that he was in a position to answer. He wasn't Spanish, to begin with, and no one in this country really cared one way or another what Frank thought regarding the treatment of *toro bravos* in Spain and whether the Spaniards were humane or not. He did think from what he'd read and heard from others that it was quite possible that there would come a day when the running of the bulls would no longer be celebrated in Pamplona. Either because bullfighting and all the events connected to it would be prohibited in Navarra, just as it had been banned in Catalonia, or more probably because towns like Pamplona would decide that staging the event for eight days in a row was just too expensive.

115

For the time being, however, and for as long as he could Frank would run. Nothing in life lasted forever and he knew that he was lucky to have discovered Pamplona and its *encierro* in time.

Once the triad had caught up with them, Frank saw that he was less than an arm's length from the hind leg of the lead bull and he touched it, for no more than a second or two and it was gone. His *encierro* was over and Frank flattened himself against the wall of the City Hall, as the rest of the herd and the runners rushed by. Ian was still in it and looked as if he was positioning himself for a run on the horns when he was knocked down by another runner. As soon as he could Frank ran over to where he'd fallen, checked that he wasn't hurt and helped him up from the ground. He was not in a good mood.

"That fucking wanker knocked me down," said Ian.

"Sure it was his fault?"

"He fucking knocked me down," said Ian, limping a bit on his left leg.

"Maybe you need to see a medic?"

"I need a coffee and then I need a drink," said Ian, and they walked to a bar with a TV where they ordered cappuccinos and croissants.

On the screen above the bar the local station was commenting on the *encierro*. Frank could see himself with his hand on the bull and then barely avoid getting steamrolled by the solid mass of runners. He also saw Ian get knocked down.

"You see," said Ian, "that little cunt tripped me."

"So he did," said Frank, "my apologies."

"Oh piss off with your apologies, Ardito, let's see what happened to the others."

"There's Peter," said Frank.

"Usual spot on Mercaderes," said Ian.

"And he's off."

The herd was running compact as it approached the curve with the first three fighting bulls that had been in the triad slamming into it. Peter was on the far side of the curve and cut in between the first three and the rest of the herd, barely missing being clipped by one of the other fighting bulls that was still on its feet and charging up Estafeta.

"Not bad," said Ian.

"There's Hector," said Frank.

"Where's his shirt?" Ian asked.

"I don't know. He had one up in the apartment, right?"

"You were with him," said Ian.

"Running barechested, imagine that, a bit of eye-candy for his feminine admirers?"

"Surprised they didn't throw him out," said Ian.

"As if, he's sober, and so long as he doesn't try running in his underwear I don't think they care. It's just the manic part of his bipolar condition."

"The what?"

"He's a manic-depressive. When he's down it's deep depression, often suicidal and then when he's up, which usually coincides with the summer, he's really up. On top of the world, you could say, able to leap tall buildings in a single bound."

117

"Superman," said Ian.

"With a super libido."

"OK, super sex."

"Endless energy is more like it. We should keep an eye on him. Just in case," said Frank.

"So, how do you know so much about this manic-depressive business?" asked Ian.

"My dad was that way."

"Gotcha."

"And Clive?" asked Frank.

"There he is," said Ian, "in the tunnel."

"Nice run."

"Very clean," Ian agreed.

"Short but sweet," said Frank. "You ready to go?"

"*Vámonos*," said Ian and they paid up and left the café.

At Bar Txoko Frank ordered two Bitches at the take-away window for himself and Ian.

"Here you go," he said, as he handed Ian his first drink of the day.

"Cheers," said Ian.

"To another run that ended well," said Frank.

As they walked to the front of the bar and Plaza Castillo they saw Clive with Peter and Hector. Irina was also there, a big surprise, for Frank at least. She was drinking something and chatting with Hector who was still barechested. Nacho was nowhere to be seen.

"Hey, I didn't think you were going to run today," said Frank after he gave her a kiss on the cheek.

"I didn't, but when I woke up I thought, hey why don't I join those guys for breakfast or drinks or both," she told him and laughed. It was strange but in part just as he had predicted. She was treating him as if nothing had happened, as if she'd never left him.

"Nothing can stop your pretty Russian," said Ian.

"Apparently not," agreed Frank.

"So, how did your run go?" asked Clive.

"Nothing heroic, was running beside one of the bulls and then stepped out of the way, near the town hall. Ask Ian how his went," said Frank.

"Oh, I know all about it. Saw a clip on the telly," said Clive.

"Forget about me," said Ian, "I'm more interested in Hector's new look."

"Yeah, what happened to your shirt, dude?" said Peter.

"I don't know really. Don't remember taking it off but once it was off it felt like the right thing to do. I really liked the feel of the cool air on my skin as I was running," said Hector, whose lean but rock solid boxer's physique seemed to glisten in the morning air.

"And you didn't feel like taking anything else off?" said Clive.

"Ha! That would've been good, a streaker at the *encierro*!" said Ian.

"Nah, just the shirt," said Hector, smiling sheepishly.

"Tomorrow's another day," said Peter.

"And another run," said Clive, trying to keep the conversation alive, but Hector didn't say anything else. He knew that at times he couldn't control himself but afterwards, after he had calmed down, he would always acknowledge his many weaknesses and wonder about whatever magic it was that made him do these things. The seasonal volcano of his unspoken desires and the way his psyche would always shake off the indecisiveness and pain of his seemingly endless emotional winters were a part of him and defined him as a man. It was not something that he could change, nor was it some sort of joke, as the others seemed to think. It was a gift and the true source of his power and virility. Still, he couldn't help but remember that nothing in life was permanent, not even his power, and that whatever had been given to him could just as easily be taken away.

Chapter 13

For breakfast Frank took Irina to the same bar where they had eaten the day before. On the way there he asked her what happened to Nacho. She told him that she didn't know, that when she woke up he was gone. It was someone else's apartment that Nacho had borrowed for the night, as he couldn't very well take Irina back to his own place. His wife was at the seaside with the kids and his mother in law. They had a vacation home there and because it was only an hour's drive from Pamplona he never knew when she might pop back in to pick up something that she'd forgotten and that she needed.

"So how did it go last night?" he asked her.

"What do you mean?"

"You know what I mean."

"Oh, you mean Nacho? Nothing much, we went for a walk."

"I know."

"You do?"

"I followed you, up past the Cathedral and the Caballo Blanco to where the two of you stopped and did what you did."

"And did you like what you saw?" she asked him with a smile. "Did it excite you?"

"Yes and no," he told her. "To be honest, it wasn't exactly what I had planned to do that night, but isn't that always how it can go in Pamplona, things can change and rapidly."

"True," she said.

"So why did you run away?"

"You really want to know why?"

"That's what I asked you," he said.

"It's because you don't own me. No one does, and you can think of what happened last night as a friendly reminder of that essential fact."

"Got it," he said. "So we're good?"

"We're good," she told him, as they found a table at the café and sat down.

"You know there's another party today at one. Should we go?" said Frank.

"*Tu eres mi capitan,*" said Irina.

"You sure about that?"

"I choose my captains," she told him. "And you are my captain."

"Whenever it suits you, you mean."

"No, you were still my captain, even last night. I just needed to make a point."

"You have a talent for the dramatic when it comes to teaching."

"I'll take that as a compliment."

"Please do," he said, although he was not at all convinced that he was her "captain" and doubted that he ever would be. Still, he could live with her lies for the time being. He was curious and wanted to see where she was taking him.

"And the party?" she asked, as a waiter came to take their orders.

"It's right outside the Caballo Blanco."

"Anyone I know?"

"Well, Anton might show up, but even if he isn't there Clive, Ian and the rest of the gang will be."

"OK."

"It's called the Norwegian party," said Frank.

"Frank?"

"Yes?"

"You should grow a beard."

"No," he told her, "I'd look like a hipster."

"But you're a painter, painters look good in beards. All the great ones had beards," she told him.

"I paint houses, it's different."

"Then do it for me," she said.

"Well, if you put it that way."

"*Gracias, mi amor.*"

"*No problema,*" he said.

"Frank."

"Yes."

"You know, all I've been doing since the *fiesta* started is eating and drinking…"

"…and running with the bulls," added Frank.

"Yet I don't think that I've gained any weight."

"You look good," he assured her.

"But that isn't possible."

"It's kinetic energy at work," he explained, "you burn calories just breathing in the air here."

"You think so?"

"It's a fact," he told her, and she laughed.

When the waiter brought their breakfasts, *huevos rancheros* for the two of them, Frank asked for a bottle of *tinto* and then pushed the basket of bread towards Irina.

"You see what I mean, everywhere I go here people are always pushing food on me," said Irina.

"It's because you're so thin."

"They want to fatten me up."

"Probably."

"So that when I have become truly *gorda* and have been killed by a handsome young matador in the bullring they'll send me to the butcher along with the rest of the *toro bravos*."

"Stands to reason, don't you think?"

"How's that?"

"Well, your meat would be very tender and as such would command a high price on the open market."

"Following a diet of chocolate, *churros*, *huevos* and Vodka tonics I guess it would," said Irina.

"An act of inspired generosity," said Frank.

"Getting fat for the slaughterhouse?"

"Because only then would the rest of this town be able to share what I have already tasted."

"Frank, that's creepy, and you haven't tasted it yet, don't forget."

"#CreepySexyDyingToTasteIt, could be the next viral hashtag."

124

"I'm sure it already exists," she said and laughed. "So tell me more about this party we're going to."

"Usual expat get together, a mix of old-timers, newbies, locals and whoever else happens to drop by."

"OK."

"You'll like it, I'm sure."

"Aye aye, captain," as the waiter brought them their bottle of red wine.

"Some wine?" said Frank.

"Absolutely," she told him, "if you want me exactly the way I was last night then I better start drinking."

"The day is long, my dear."

"I mean it, Frank, I'm gonna go crazy on you again," she told him with a mischievous smile.

"Fire away," he told her, "but this time I'm not going to stand by and watch."

"Aye aye, *mon capitaine*."

When they finished their eggs and were ready to go Irina asked if they could take the bottle of wine outside.

"We could sneak it out. You could conceal it under that shirt that Nacho lent you," he said and laughed, because even though she had tied the lower part of the shirt in a knot to show off her hips and bare midriff it was still huge.

"It's certainly big enough."

"You don't want any more bread before we leave?" said Frank.

"Still fattening me up?"

125

"Finish that last piece and we'll go."

"You first," she said and laughed.

***

Outside the party was in full swing. There were perhaps a hundred people standing around the tree and the table where the food and drinks were being served. He saw Clive and Hector and Peter and many others whose faces were familiar but whose names he couldn't remember. Walking over to the table he introduced Irina to two Swedes, Sven and Eric, who he'd never met before but who were chatting with Dave, the barman from the International Gutter Club party.

"So how were the bullfights yesterday?" asked Dave.

"Great," said Frank.

"And the girls, how did they take it as a first experience?"

"Not bad, I'd say, although the American kept insisting that it was unfair."

"I see she's not here today."

"Her boyfriend finally tracked her down at the Club where we were dancing around midnight."

"A happy ending," said Dave, turning his head to look at Irina as she chatted with the two Swedes.

"And your Russian beauty?"

"Better than ever," said Frank.

"She wouldn't happen to have any sisters older than eighteen, would she?"

"None that I know of but in case she discovers one I'll let you know."

"Much obliged, Mr. Ardito."

"*De nada, hombre.*"

"They've got beer and wine and even champagne at the table if you're thirsty," said Dave.

Frank walked over to the crowd of people around the table who were busy laughing, drinking and eating, and he saw someone he knew who was helping out.

"Betty," he said, waving to a short woman who was about his age or perhaps a bit older. She was a Norwegian who lived in New York City and had been coming to the *fiesta* for twenty years at least.

"Frank!" she called out. "I'm surrounded. Climb under the table if you need something."

"Just two glasses of wine and I'll be on my way," said Frank who crawled under one of the foldout picnic tables and then stood up next to Betty who wrapped her arms around him and gave him a kiss on the lips.

"Well, that's quite the welcome," said Frank.

"Has it really been a year?" said Betty.

"Pretty much."

"It's amazing how fast twelve months can pass, but how are you? You look good."

"Can't complain."

"You here alone?"

"No," he told her.

"Didn't think so. Who's the lucky lady?"

"She's standing next to Dave and those two Swedes."

"Pretty, way too pretty for you, Ardito. Can't imagine what she sees in you," she told him and laughed.

"Luck of the forty-somethings, perhaps?"

"Doubt it," she said with a smile. "So what's her name?"

"Irina."

"Of course, Russian."

"How's that?"

"Beautiful country, beautiful women."

"OK, you approve of my new flame, can I have some of that red wine, please?"

"*Sí, señor*," she told him and handed him two glasses.

"Thanks, Betty."

"Bring her over here when you can," she said, as he made his way through the crowd and around the tree to get back to Irina. Frank had to be careful with the glasses because of the friends who would suddenly recognize him and hit him on the back or the shoulders causing the wine to spill out over his fingers and onto his white Converse sneakers. All of the shirts and painter's pants that were a part of Frank's Pamplona wardrobe were irretrievably stained with wine, *patxaran* and other drinks. Anything that he took to the *fiesta* spotless never came home that way. For this reason he always admired the locals who would show up at these parties in immaculately cleaned and pressed button down white cotton shirts and trousers.

Doing what he could to protect his drinks, Frank eventually made it back to where Irina was standing and handed her a glass.

"Hey Frank," said Peter, who along with Hector was standing next to Irina.

Everyone was listening to one of the Swedes who was telling what happened to him last night when he'd gone to move his car, which was in the underground parking of Plaza Castillo.

"It was past midnight and like everyone else here I'd been out drinking but I didn't think that driving while thoroughly drunk would be much of a problem as I didn't have far to go."

As he explained it, he was just going to move it to another parking lot that was on the other side of the river, one where you didn't have to pay any money. So he took the staircase in Plaza Castillo down into the enormous multi-level parking garage and started looking for his car. Certainly not the easiest thing to do after a night of bar hopping and tequila shots, especially considering that he couldn't remember where exactly he'd parked it. All he knew was that it was wedged in between a van and a concrete pillar. After exploring two levels he finally found his VW Golf and pressed the button on his keys to unlock the doors. The lights blinked on and off. Everything was normal and he opened the door, sat down, buckled up and put the key in the ignition. The diesel engine started and he pressed down on the gas pedal a couple of times to warm it up and was about to release the parking brake when he saw these three guys standing up behind his car and banging on his rear window.

"What the hell, I said to myself," said Sven.

"Who were they?" asked Irina.

"Three Spanish kids from Malaga who had taken a train up from the South to see the *fiesta* for the first time. But they hadn't planned anything. It was totally spur of the moment and they thought they could sleep in the grass but then they heard all these stories about people being robbed out in the park so they went underground."

"Jesus, down in that garage, they were sleeping there?" said Hector.

"Yeah, they had sleeping bags and stuff to drink and smoke and even bread to make sandwiches," said Sven.

"Rugged," said Frank.

"The air down there is fucking toxic," said Hector.

"True," said Sven, "but they're young and you do crazy things when you're young, right?"

"If they get drunk enough, they won't even notice the difference," said Peter, and everyone laughed.

"You should have seen 'em," said Sven, "they were standing there in their underwear with this kind of happy, drunk, totally wasted look on their faces. They had been at it for two days, I think, without any sleep and I had interrupted them just when they were getting ready to call it a night."

"That's the spirit," said Hector.

"We should drink to their courage and perhaps their good health," said Peter.

"Nah, we should just drink," said Frank, who finished his glass in one gulp and asked Irina if she needed a refill.

"Might as well," she told him and he walked over to the table again. This time there were plastic cups of red wine set out for anyone who wanted some and he took two. On his way back he saw that Nacho had joined the group along with Ian and Anton.

"Ardito, you wanker, do you ever do anything else besides get pissed?" said Ian.

"Never, abstinence is bad for my Pamplona voice," said Frank, as he handed Irina her new cup of wine.

"That usually comes around the third or fourth day," said Ian.

"What's Pamplona voice?" said Anton.

"Well, that's when you've been drinking non-stop for three or four days and nights and your vocal chords pretty much shut down until you take a breather," said Frank.

"And you'll notice that's usually about half way through the *fiesta*," said Peter.

"Right, when people take a *siesta* from the *fiesta*,'" said Frank.

"*Claro*," said Nacho. "We're only human." And Frank looked at him and thought, he doesn't know that I know. He's in a good mood, and why shouldn't he be. He spent the whole night fucking Irina.

"But until that moment arrives," said Frank, still looking at Nacho, "abstinence is a sin."

"Well, no one is telling you to stop," said Anton.

"And where have you been?" said Frank.

"A long story, my friend."

"Which you'll have to tell me some day."

"One day when I'm drunk enough," said Anton.

131

"More women with angry boyfriends?"

"Worse."

"I'm curious, let's hear it," said Frank.

"When I've had enough to drink," said Anton, blushing.

Frank looked at Hector and saw that the bruise on his face appeared to be a little less livid. He was standing next to Irina and the two of them were a study in contrasts, one dark and muscular and the other elegantly slender and unblemished. Hector had put a shirt on, a red tank top that accentuated his boxer's physique.

"Ardito," said Ian.

"Yes."

"Do you need tickets for today's *corrida*?"

"Maybe, who are the matadors?" asked Frank.

"I don't know, but the bulls you met this morning," said Ian.

"True enough," said Frank.

"Just you and your hottie?"

"Just us."

"Thirty euros," said Ian.

"Usual nosebleed seats?"

"Well, the good thing about nosebleed seats is that if the Arena ever collapses you'll be on top of the situation."

"Wonderful," said Frank, who was reaching for his wallet when Nacho stopped him and said, "Come with us."

"Sounds like you might have a better deal," said Peter.

"I certainly can't beat his prices," said Ian, who pretended to be miffed at the loss of a sale but who in fact could care less. He was drinking, he felt good and the prospects of running into other parties on the horizon with free booze were excellent.

"If you insist," said Frank.

"And after the *corrida* the *peña* is organizing a dinner and you're both invited."

"*Perfecto*," said Frank.

"So, I'll see the two of you in front of the clubhouse at around five-thirty, *vale?*"

"We'll be there," said Frank. As Irina's chosen captain he understood that he was her man but that he needed to be more curious and elastic. He needed to follow her and observe and to not impede whatever fate had in store for them on any given night. That was what she wanted, thought Frank, but not necessarily what she would get.

They left the party at around a quarter to five, more or less when everyone else who was going to the *corrida* started to remember that they did have tickets and that it would take them a while to get through the crowds and the bars that they would walk by and where they would be seen by other friends who would then pull them in for a drink or two.

After taking their time and stopping for a few selfies against the wall with the mountains on the outskirts of the city in the background, Frank and Irina arrived at the clubhouse just as the *peña* started its procession down Calle del Carmen in the direction of Estafeta.

"There's Nacho," said Irina.

"I see him," said Frank, "and I think he sees us." The band was playing and Frank could barely hear what Irina was saying. Nacho waved and they waved back.

"For a second I was beginning to think that you had changed your plans," said Nacho, when Frank and Irina had joined him at the head of the procession.

"No new plans," said Frank, "we wouldn't miss it for the world."

"I like your friends," said Nacho.

"The guys at the party?"

"Yes, the Americans and that crazy looking Scot."

"Ian's quite the character."

"But the Americans, too, were different. Not at all what you usually see during the *fiesta*," said Nacho.

"How so?" asked Frank.

"Well, the smaller one, I'm guessing of course, but just by looking at him I'd say that he was a soldier somewhere not too long ago."

"True."

"But the other one is stranger still, the one with the red undershirt."

"He has his moments," Frank agreed.

"He is built like an athlete but is quite vulnerable and set to go off like the soldier, just in a different way."

"My time bomb friends," said Frank, "you're batting a thousand today, Nacho."

"Batting a thousand?"

"American expression, means you nailed it."

"I nailed it. I like that."

"They both are passionate about running with the bulls," said Frank. "Maybe that has something to do with their strangeness?"

"You run with the bulls, too, don't you Frank? But you're not like them."

"No, I guess I'm not."

"But you understand them," said Nacho.

"Kind of, kind of not."

"*Vosotros sois hermanos*," you are brothers, he said.

"We are, I guess."

"But you're the brother who protects them."

"I do what?"

"Because you understand, Frank."

"No, I beg to differ here, Nacho. One is an ex Navy Seal and the other was a semi-professional boxer. In short, they're quite capable of taking care of themselves, thank you. But don't worry. It's OK. In fact, everything's OK. It's *fiesta* and we're on our way to the *corrida*," said Frank, who was vaguely disturbed by what Nacho had just told him. Peter and Hector were his friends, yes, and time bombs without a doubt but that was not his problem. Frank had seen this happen to other people, his father included, and when either Peter or Hector did finally explode he would not take the blame because he knew that there was fuck all that anyone could do to stop a bomb when it was about to blow. He had never been able to stop his father in all the years that he had

135

known him. Nor had he ever been able to protect himself as a teenager from his father's manic periods. The only souvenirs that he had managed to preserve from his youth and save from the drunken rage of his father's mood swings were the memories of how it had been when he was a young boy and had looked up to his father as a kind of god, perfect and forgiving, strong and someone who would always be there for him. A veritable hero, up until the day he killed himself with a pistol that he'd borrowed from a neighbor.

Nacho, thought Frank, was fundamentally a nice guy but he didn't know shit.

Chapter 14

The *corrida* was something of a bust with mediocre bulls, missed opportunities and failed *faenas* on the part of the first two matadors. The last matador, however, made up for his colleagues. His *faena*, which was elegant and subdued and yet full of risk-taking, reminded everyone that the objective of any good matador was to create art. It also helped the crowd forget the ugly kills that had been thoroughly botched and that had taken forever and that at times were enough to make even the most passionate *aficionado* a card carrying member of PETA.

At the end of the *corrida,* as the last matador stood ready to kill his second bull, he had put behind him a *faena* that had once again thrilled the *aficionados* with a series of passes that brought the bull closer and closer until it seemed that there was nothing that separated his slender body from the animal's deadly horns. His inspired performances that afternoon took everyone by surprise. He had been a relative underachiever in the world of bullfighting and it was as if he had woken up that morning and decided "I am a great matador, and today will be my day."

His kill was quick and precise with his sword going exactly where he willed it to go, to that one spot that would take it through the bull's *morillo* and down into its heart. The animal fell to its knees and died almost as soon as he had finished. The Arena roared its approval and the *torero* was awarded two ears and a ceremonial lap around the ring on the shoulders of one of the men in his group.

"Why is he being carried around like that?" Irina asked Frank.

"Because he was so good the president of the jury gave him two ears and two ears gets you a lap around the ring. It's a great honor," said Frank.

"And shouldn't you be carrying me around Pamplona after my performance last night?"

"Your performance?" he said, laughing and almost spitting out the wine that he was drinking.

"You know."

"Of course, you might have a point, but instead of carrying you around the ring maybe I should be spanking you?"

"Ha!"

"But you see how he holds the ears up?"

"I do."

"Well, where are we going to get a pair of ears like that?" asked Frank.

"Good question," said Irina.

"They're not exactly things you can pick up in the meat section of your local supermarket."

"What if we make them on our own, you know with papier-mâché and wires and stuff?"

"Perhaps," said Frank.

"I think, though, that we should first practice just you carrying me on your shoulders."

"You're light, it's not a problem."

"True, but still you won't really know if you can until you try it," said Irina.

"OK," said Frank, lowering himself so that Irina could climb on to his shoulders. "Hang on."

"What are you two doing?" said Nacho, laughing and looking up at Irina who was waving her arms in the air.

"Practicing for the day when Frank carries me around Pamplona," said Irina.

"*Claro*," said Nacho, just as the first of the ice-cubes and sangria hit the three of them, especially Irina. The clean shirt that Nacho had given her was now splattered pink.

"Having fun up there?" said Frank.

"It's great, you should try it," Irina told him.

"The party's over," said Nacho, as the *peñas* started to hop over the barriers and into the ring. All the doors of the tunnel had been opened and everyone was filing out through the main entrance.

"Now we go to eat?" said Frank.

"We go to eat," said Nacho.

It took them a while to get there, but no one seemed to be in a hurry. All the *peña* bands were playing at the same time and none of the bands ever played what another was playing even if they were standing right next to each other. Anarchy as usual reigned supreme, and adding to the music there was the noise of thousands of people on Estafeta shouting to be heard, or talking or laughing, plus the occasional traveling drum troupe. It was the usual crazy mix of decibels on any

139

street in the *Casco Viejo* at the end of another long day and the beginning of an even longer night.

At times the going was so slow they were able to squeeze into a bar, order a drink, watch the bartender make the drink and then get out in time to catch the group before it had traveled too far into the blob of people in the street. They did this three times and in the last bar they met Eneko who had two women at his side, both of them much younger than he was. He was telling them some funny story which made them laugh a lot and when he said "that's it, I've finished" they objected and insisted that it wasn't finished and that perhaps after he'd ordered them another round of Gin and tonics it would truly be finished.

"*Cabrón!*" he shouted when he saw Frank and Irina come into the bar.

"Eneko," said Frank, as his friend lifted him off the ground in one of his bear hugs.

"Frank, are you happy with this *fiesta?*" he asked.

"I am," said Frank, with his feet dangling in the air.

"No, tell me the truth, are you deliriously happy?"

"Bordering on delirious," said Frank, his feet still off the ground.

"He's a good man," said Eneko to Irina, "but should you have any problems with him, here's my number."

"*Gracias,*" said Irina, as Eneko released Frank from his embrace and handed Irina his card.

"Hate to hug and run," said Frank, as he paid the bartender and grabbed his drink, "but we've gotta go."

"*Cabrón*! *Te quiero*!" said Eneko to Frank.

"Why does he keep calling you *cabrón*?" asked Irina once they were outside.

"It's his term of endearment," said Frank.

"What does it mean?"

"Loosely translated, asshole."

"Nice," she said and laughed. They had just turned right on Mercaderes and were now walking uphill towards the clubhouse.

"As I'm sure you could tell, he's a different kind of friend," said Frank.

"Very different," Irina agreed.

"Nacho, what's on the menu tonight?"

"*Tienes hambre, amigo*?" said Nacho.

"*Sí, señor.*"

"Don't worry, whatever it is that our cooks have planned, you won't be disappointed."

Indeed, what the chefs of the *peña* had prepared was nothing short of a medieval feast. In a meeting hall adjacent to the kitchen they had set up five long tables, each of which had room for twenty-five people. There were already platters of white asparagus and *pimientos rellanos de manitas y hongos* (piquillo peppers stuffed with pigs' trotters and porcini mushrooms) as antipasti along with mouth-watering *chistorra* (a Navarran sausage) in a red sauce.

"Try a bit of everything," said Nacho, who was sitting between Frank and Irina.

141

"Oh, this looks tasty," said Irina, forking a piece of *chistorra* on to her plate.

"Pass me that basket of bread," said Nacho to Frank.

"Got it," said Frank, "here you go."

"Thanks," said Nacho, placing the breadbasket in front of Irina.

"The white asparagus are fantastic," said Frank.

"The stuffed red peppers, don't forget those," said Nacho.

"Absolutely not," said Frank.

"*Vino?*" said Nacho to Irina, as he poured a Navarran red from a decanter.

"*Sí, gracias.*"

"*Y tu?*" said Nacho to Frank.

"*Por supuesto* (of course)."

"Just remember," said Nacho, "this is just the antipasto, then there's the first dish, the second, the dessert, various liquors and coffee plus whatever bars we'll end up in after this."

"In short, they'll have to roll us out of here," said Frank.

"Pretty much," said Nacho.

"I don't mind, drag me wherever you want to go and when I fall asleep just prop me up against a wall and I'll be fine," said Irina, as she put another stuffed red pepper on her plate.

After the antipasti were finished bowls of *pochas* (white bean soup) were brought out from the kitchen and served to everyone sitting at the tables.

"Have you ever tried this, Frank?" asked Nacho.

"I have indeed, one of my favorites."

"And you, Irina?" said Nacho.

"First time."

"Then you're in for a treat."

"It smells delicious," said Irina.

Nacho made sure that Irina's wine glass was always full. There was a lot of chatter in the room and for the most part he spoke with Frank but every now and then he would whisper something into Irina's ear that would make her laugh.

The second course had two different dishes, *Rabo de toro deshuesado con clavo relleno de tuétano* (Boned bulltail with clove stuffed with marrow) and *Gorrín* (Suckling pig).

"*Mamma mia,*" said Frank when the second course platters were brought to the table, "this is impressive."

"Wait 'til you taste it, my friend," said Nacho.

The piglet, Frank discovered, was excellent and the meat on the bull's tail was so tender that it seemed to almost melt in his mouth.

"So?" asked Nacho, looking at Frank.

"Suffice it to say that this is a great dinner. Many thanks to you, Nacho, for having us here."

"*Un placer.*" (my pleasure)

"And what's for dessert?" asked Irina.

"A surprise," said Nacho.

"I like the sound of that," said Irina.

"Here it comes," said Nacho.

Trays carrying wooden mugs filled with a white substance that looked like custard were brought in from the kitchen.

143

"It's called *Cuajada* and it's a very antique dessert typical of Navarra. It's made from goat's milk and usually topped with honey or nuts, or both."

"Delicious," said Irina after her first spoonful.

"Amazing," said Frank, "everything, just amazing."

"Remember, there's still the *patxaran* and the other liquors," said Nacho.

"I could die and go to heaven now," said Frank.

"Bliss," said Irina, as she savored each spoonful.

"Traditional dishes, that's what we do best," said Nacho.

After dessert, they were offered espressos, *patxaran* or cognac.

"I'm stuffed," said Frank.

"So what now?" asked Irina.

"Well, we can stay here and chat or leave and see what the night has to offer," said Nacho.

"I say we go for a walk," said Frank.

"Then let's go," said Nacho, and they got up from the table taking their dishes with them to the kitchen as they left.

***

Outside on the street the air was cool and dry and the sky above them was clear. It was a windy night and because Irina said that she was cold they stopped at a store on Estafeta where Frank bought her a red hoodie.

"The weather in Pamplona, or Mordor as we sometimes refer to it, is unpredictable because of the mountains," said Nacho, "and so my dear Irina, during the *fiesta*, even if it's blazing hot at noon it's never a bad idea to have a sweatshirt with you at night. It's a desert here in the summer, or rather, it can be."

They walked up Calle de la Chapitela, past Hotel La Perla, thinking that they would try the clubs again. They didn't even look to see if anyone was at Bar Windsor. Ian, however, saw them and shouted out to Frank.

"Ardito, you wanker!"

"Hey Ian," said Frank.

"As he blithely walks right by his mates and not even so much as a How Do You Fucking Do. Me thinks that woman has gone to your head, Ardito," said Ian, waving them over to their table.

"We just came from a dinner with the Irrintzi *peña*," said Irina.

"Well then you're entitled to another drink, young lady," said Ian, grabbing a chair from another table so that she could sit next to him.

"So where's your alter-ego, Clive?" asked Frank.

"He'll be here, or at least that's what he said. We think he's found a new girlfriend. Another woman that he'll propose to but never marry."

"Hey Frank, what's up?" said Peter, who was sitting next to Hector.

"Not much."

145

"There are some seats over here," said Hector, and Frank and Irina sat next to Hector while Nacho took the seat that Ian had reserved for Irina.

"We were just talking about the run tomorrow and thinking that maybe we should all run Mercaderes for a change," said Peter.

"Why not?" said Frank.

"Of course, that's the curve," said Ian.

"Leads right into it," said Frank.

"And we didn't know if your lady friend was up to running it," said Ian.

"Why don't you ask her?"

"Madame Irina," said Ian, standing up and with his right arm, holding his beer, outstretched in her direction, "would you care to join us tomorrow morning on the curve?"

"Is that the part where the bulls slam into the wall?" she asked.

"Not always."

"Tell her the truth, Ian," said Peter.

"Well, sometimes."

"The truth," said Hector.

"OK, it's fifty-fifty."

"Try about ninety percent of the time," said Frank.

"Well, I could, but I don't know if I'll get up when Frank does," said Irina.

"Not a problem," said Ian.

"How's that?" said Frank.

146

"She can sleep with me," Ian said, and Frank looked at him and then laughed.

"Hi Frank," said Clive, as he appeared from out of the crowd in Plaza Castillo with a new flame, a tall blonde, and walked over to their table. "What are you guys drinking, I'm going to the bar."

"Vodka tonic," said Irina.

"I'll have a Rum Collins," said Frank.

"Same as Irina," said Nacho.

"Oh guys, this is Ilse. She wants to run with us tomorrow and she's from Amsterdam."

"Fine, fine, the more the merrier," said Ian, as he pulled another two chairs from the table next to theirs and squeezed them in between himself and Nacho.

"By the way, don't worry about the bulls slamming into the curve, we don't start from that side. Only Ian pulls that kind of crap," said Hector, looking at Irina and at her legs and taking a sip from his tequila cocktail.

"Well, that's good to hear, just in case I do manage to get up in time," said Irina.

"Have you ever run before?" said Ilse to Irina.

"Just once, the first day."

"Someone wanted me to run with them today but I saw the first run on the seventh and said NO WAY. It's crazy," said Ilse, as she tied her long blonde hair in a ponytail.

"But Clive said you want to run tomorrow," said Irina.

147

"I do. He told me that, yes, it is crazy but also a lot of fun so I agreed to run with him."

"Well, that's a leap of faith," said Hector.

"Or a lover's leap," said Peter.

"Is this your first time in Pamplona?" asked Ian.

"Very first," said Ilse.

"And what do you think?"

"I love it!"

"The curve is exciting," said Peter, "you'll enjoy it."

"I'm sure I will," said Ilse.

"Here comes your Prince Charming," said Ian. Clive was carrying a tray with five cocktails.

"Sorry it took me so long," said Clive, "that place is always packed." He put the tray on the table and passed around the drinks.

"Next round is on me," said Frank.

"Good, because I'm going to run out of money soon if I don't find a cashpoint around here that works."

"There's one right across the Plaza," said Hector.

"Where?" said Clive.

"It's hard to see. I'll show you where it is if you want."

"Thanks."

"No problem," said Hector.

Clive then whispered something into Ilse's ear that made her laugh and Hector told Peter to keep an eye on his cocktail.

The ATM was next to a shop that was selling San Fermin t-shirts, and if you didn't know where you were going it was easy to miss it.

"Are you sure it's here?" said Clive.

"Have faith, my eyes are like night vision goggles," Hector told him.

"Good for you, I can't see a goddamn thing."

"Here it is," said Hector, when they stopped and he pointed to it.

"Doesn't look like they're terribly interested in doing business," said Clive.

"I guess not," said Hector.

Clive withdrew his daily limit, put the cash in his wallet and said, "Let's go."

"I told you it was there," said Hector.

"They should have installed it as a braille version for the blind," said Clive, and they both laughed. As they continued to make jokes about the "braille cashpoint", they were passing by Café Iruña on their way across the Plaza when a tall man with long black hair deliberately bumped into Clive and Hector while a young boy walking behind them stole Clive's wallet out of his back pocket.

"You fucking Americans," said the man in heavily accented English, "get out of my way."

"My wallet," said Clive, "fuck, that little kid's nicked my wallet."

"I'm on him," said Hector, darting off across the Plaza in pursuit of the thief. The gypsy kid tried to avoid capture heading for the thickest part of the crowd that was watching a Spanish rock band play in the center of the square. He was dressed in white and red like everyone else, but Hector had him in his sights and could already see who he was going to hand the wallet to. There was another gypsy kid near Bar Txoko, waiting his turn to receive the baton in this relay that would carry Clive's wallet and his cash to their adult handler.

"Oh no you don't," said Hector to himself, as he raced after the kid. "You are so not going to do that."

The thief reached the edge of the crowd and kept running towards Bar Txoko where the other boy was standing with his hand outstretched waiting to grab the wallet. He could see Hector sprinting after his friend and shouted something to the boy in a language that Hector couldn't understand.

"That ain't gonna help your sorry ass," said Hector, who reached out and grabbed the gypsy thief by the shirt only to see him toss the wallet to his friend who promptly disappeared down one of the streets that led to the bullring.

"Fuck!" shouted Hector when he saw that not only did the accomplice escape with Clive's wallet but also the one who he had chased across the Plaza had disappeared as well. "Fuck it! Fucking, fuck, fucked! I almost had that little shit."

"Did you get the wallet?" said Clive, out of breath and panting after his race across the Plaza Castillo.

"It's gone," said Hector, "there were two of them, a sort of gypsy Olympic relay team."

"Damn it, that had all my cards, my driver's license! Everything! Fuck!"

"You can say that again."

"I gotta make some phone calls," said Clive, who perhaps seeing the humor in the situation started to laugh.

"Yep, you sure do," said Hector, who for some reason started to laugh with him.

"One hell of a sprint," said Clive.

"Good practice for tomorrow's *encierro,*" said Hector.

"Little shits," said Clive, and then, "who gives a goddamn!", and he laughed again.

"Fuck 'em," said Hector.

"That's right, fuck 'em."

"Here, I'll buy you a drink," said Hector and they walked into Txoko together, laughing all the way to the bar and no worse for the wear and tear.

Chapter 15

Back at the Windsor the others waited in vain for Hector and ·
Clive, as everyone continued chatting and ordering round after round of
beers, tequila shots and cocktails. Then when two o'clock came and
went Irina decided that it was time to go dancing in the Basque bars and
asked both Nacho and Frank to choose who would accompany her.

"Shall we flip a coin?" asked Nacho.

"Heads I win, tails she's yours," said Frank, as he pulled a euro
out of his pocket and flipped it into the air.

"Tails!" said Irina, who caught it and showed them both the
one-euro coin with the bust of the new King of Spain.

"Looks like she's yours," said Frank to Nacho, with an
expression of one who was not amused.

"Why so sad?" she told Frank. "I was only joking. I want you
both to come with me."

"Good one," said Nacho, smiling at her joke. Frank pretended to
smile too, but in reality he was wondering when Irina was going to
come to her senses and treat him as the captain she said he was. Even
though he agreed that she was probably right about the other night when
she said that he needed to learn a lesson, he was growing tired of her
bait and switch tactics and thought to himself that she'd already made
her point and that making it again and again was just overkill. Still, he
had only met her a few days ago and in spite of whatever he may have
thought about their first meeting in the real world she was just another
young woman who was still checking him out as well as checking out a

152

number of other men. That was pretty much the norm in Pamplona, or anywhere else for that matter, and if what she had in mind was a threesome with him and Nacho, then to have her, or at least a part of her, he would go along with it.

Not too far from the City Hall there was a street which was full of nothing but what Frank and his Anglo friends usually referred to as the "Basque bars" and which during the *fiesta* was the place to go if you wanted dark, loud and sweaty locales where you could pretty much do whatever you wanted to do with anyone else there who happened to be on your same booze infused wavelength. The first bar they hit was long and narrow except for the rear, which had a dance floor that was a few feet higher than the rest of the locale. It was packed with what looked to be teenagers and twenty-somethings and walking in made Frank feel as if he were in a tunnel. Nacho was leading the way with Irina right behind him and Frank pulling up the rear and holding on to Irina's skirt. Except for the shirt she was wearing exactly what she'd worn the day before when he had watched her with Nacho in the grass.

Frank ordered three Vodka tonics from the bar, as they slowly made their way to the dance floor.

"Here," he said to Nacho and Irina when the drinks were ready. "A nosotros!" (to us), and they raised their plastic cups and saluted their group. After that they danced for a while and when they had had enough of that bar they ordered some more drinks and marched off to the next one.

"So," said Nacho to Irina when they were out on the street again, "are you having a good time?"

153

"Yes," she told him, "but I want to dance some more."

"We're going to another place."

"Where we can dance?" she asked.

"Yes," he said.

"All of us?"

"Por supuesto," he told her, and she reached out for his hand. Irina liked Frank but she felt that Nacho was softer, altogether more compatible with her idea of eroticism. With Frank it was hard for Irina to say exactly what it was that made her hold back. Perhaps it was his impatience and the constant anger, almost rage, that she could feel bubbling just beneath the surface of his emotions. Whatever the case she wasn't ready for him alone, not yet.

Frank looked at Irina as they went in to the next bar and while she wasn't swaying or falling into anything she was already at that point where she wouldn't have been able to make it back to the apartment without someone to lead the way. She was in a playful mood and kissing Nacho and Frank and just about everyone else she met in the new bar while dancing. After a while they got another round of Vodka tonics and hit the road again.

"Where are we going?" she asked.

"Back to the apartment," said Frank. By then she was walking between the two of them, with her arms on their shoulders and their hands around her slender waist to keep her from tripping on the cobblestones.

"But I'm not tired," she protested.

"That's good," said Frank.

"Why?" she asked.

"Because we're going back to the apartment," Frank explained.

"All of us?"

"Yes, all of us."

"Good," she told him, "because I want you both with me."

"No worries," said Frank, when the three of them stood in front of the entrance to his building.

"I've got an unopened bottle of Laphroaig Scotch upstairs, but no ice," said Frank.

"Who needs ice," said Nacho.

"In fact, I didn't think you'd mind."

They then pretty much carried Irina up to the apartment, lifting her into the air or letting her use her feet when she felt like it and insisted that she was perfectly capable of walking, even if she was tripping over two out of every three of the steps that she took.

When they got to the front of Frank's flat he let everyone in and then he went to get the bottle of Laphroaig from the kitchen. When he walked into the living room with the bottle and three shot glasses Irina and Nacho were kissing on the couch.

"Hey, not so fast you two, I haven't even opened the Scotch yet," said Frank.

"The party's already begun, Frank," said Nacho, as he put his hand under Irina's shirt and undid her bra.

"Here, have a drink," said Frank to Irina after he opened the bottle and handed her one of the shot glasses. She downed it in one go and asked for another.

"Thirsty, yes?"

"I want to dance," she said, once Nacho had removed her shirt and bra, "put on some music, dance music."

"OK," said Frank, "I'll find you something." He got his phone and looked through the music library and chose a selection of Cuban Salsa that was current and danceable. By the time he set up the phone Irina had already taken off her skirt and slip and was dancing nude in front of the two of them with the bottle of Laphroaig in her hand.

"So, what are you guys waiting for?" said Irina, looking at Frank and Nacho who were still dressed.

"Guess we were just admiring your good looks," said Frank.

"Well, I'm waiting," she said, and the two of them got naked and joined her, passing the bottle around, kissing her on her breasts and neck, her hips and her *fondoschiena*. She was taking it all in and feeling their power, much as the runners did when they touched the bulls on the corner of Estafeta. She let them do whatever they wanted to do. She was the goddess of the night's pagan rite and they were her parishioners feasting on her generosity as they took her alone or together for what seemed forever until they collapsed on the floor just before dawn.

Chapter 16

Clive awoke on the morning of the ninth of July in the grassy area where the Norwegians had held their party, just in front of the Caballo Blanco. The last thing he could remember was dancing in a club near the bullring at around half past two. Before that he had visited many bars, some with Hector and some not. Not having any cash or cards Clive was totally dependent on Hector's generosity and then, when Hector had disappeared, Clive's *noche loca* continued with the drinks and *tapas* that others both aquaintences and strangers offered him. That had gone on until he had blacked out and ended up, exactly how he couldn't recall, in the wet grass.

He checked his pockets and discovered that he still had the keys to his apartment, which meant that he could go there and change and even have a shower. But then he looked at his watch and saw that it was late and realized that the others would be waiting for him at Ian's place on Estafeta.

Better to meet up with the group, he thought. He reached for his phone to give Ian a call, to tell him that he was on his way, but the battery was dead.

When he stood up he had a slight headache and his right leg was sore. A hangover and stiff muscles, however, were minor inconveniences and would pass soon enough. What was a problem, and one that would not resolve itself on its own, was his urgent need for a strong coffee.

"Patience," he told himself, "you'll get there."

When he rounded the corner at Mercaderes and started walking up Estafeta he could almost taste the horrible coffee from Ian's coffee machine. Just about anything was palatable when you're an addict, he thought.

Coming up on the entrance to Ian's building he saw Hector speaking into the intercom. He was still wearing the same dirty shirt and trousers but looked as if he'd managed to sleep a few hours.

"Hector!" he called out.

"Hey Clive," said Hector, as the door opened, "where did you go last night?"

"Good question. I don't remember everything."

"One of those nights," said Hector, as they walked through the hall to the stairs.

"One to remember, if I only could remember," said Clive, smiling.

"Ouch, oh well, at least you were able to go to your place and sleep a bit."

"In theory yes, but I fell asleep outside."

"Outstanding," said Hector, as they walked up the stairs together, "I didn't get back to my place either, got sidetracked by a pair of pretty Mexicans."

Clive could hear voices coming from the apartment as they approached the landing. Hector rang the doorbell, but instead of Ian or Peter or Frank the Dutch girl opened the door. It was only then, in fact, that Clive remembered that he had left her at Bar Windsor with the others.

158

"Ilse," said Clive, visibly embarrassed and yet at the same time thinking that extenuating circumstances were just that, extenuating circumstances.

"Clive," she said, with an expression that told him that she wasn't angry, curious perhaps, but on the whole in a forgiving mood.

"Good morning," said Hector. "Any coffee inside there?"

"It's where it always is," shouted Ian from the living room.

As Hector took the lead, Clive said that he was sorry to Ilse.

"For what," she asked.

"For disappearing like that."

"Oh, don't worry about it."

"Really?"

"I heard about those gypsy kids, it would've upset me, too," said Ilse, "anyway, your friend Peter explained everything and we had a lovely evening together."

"You did?"

"Sure, he's a lot of fun," said Ilse.

"I bet he is," said Clive, who was relieved that she had been chaperoned but who wasn't at all sure that Peter had limited his activities to being a chaperon. But that was a problem, assuming that he actually cared who she slept with, which he could think about later on. What mattered now was the *encierro*.

Once in the living room he saw that Frank and Irina were there too.

"Hey," said Peter, "we heard about your heroic chase with the gypsy kids. Did you ever find them?"

159

"No, Peter, we did not, but on the other hand I had a wild night *con mi hermano* Hector."

"We heard about that, too," said Peter.

"The news of my run-in with the gypsy kids travels fast," said Clive.

"We met some of the same people who were taking care of your various tabs around town," said Peter. "You always seemed tó be one step ahead of us."

"But at least we know that throughout the night our wanker bullfighter was OK," said Ian.

"Your concern is touching," said Clive, smiling, as he finally poured himself a cup of coffee from the machine.

"So, who's running today?" asked Ian.

"All of us," said Frank.

"No, I mean the bulls."

"Miura," said Hector.

"That's strange, they usually have them on the last day, the fourteenth, when all the French arrive," said Peter.

"I guess they decided to mix it up this year," said Frank.

"No worries, lads," said Ian, "it won't be the first time we've run with them."

"If none of them go *suelto* they stay together, and if you stay out of their way they positively love you," said Peter.

"Bull in the hole love, it's the best, admit it, Hector," said Ian, "tell me I'm wrong."

"You're wrong, you're always wrong," said Hector, as he looked at yesterday's *encierro* pics in the Diario de Navarra.

"Someone turn on the telly," said Ian.

"TVE?" asked Frank.

"What else."

Frank found the channel and turned the volume up. There were shots of the runners still waiting down at the City Hall and views of the Miuras standing in the corral at the beginning of Santo Domingo.

"Man, are they ever big," said Hector, looking up from the newspaper.

"How the hell they ever manage to kill those monsters is beyond me," said Peter.

"Just think of the *cojones* those matadors have," said Frank.

"You couldn't pay me to get in a ring with one of them," said Peter.

"Well, they pay them, they pay them a lot," said Clive.

"Still sure you want to run with those babies," said Peter to Ilse.

"I'm not afraid."

"Good for you," said Peter.

"What time is it?" said Ian.

"Almost ten to eight," said Clive.

"Tell me when they start to move," said Ian, who was offering everyone a sheet of yesterday's Diario to roll into a baton.

"So we're all going to run the curve today?" asked Peter.

"We're in," said Frank, speaking for himself and Irina.

"Absolutely," said Hector.

161

"Of course," said Clive.

"Ian, they've opened up the barriers, they're moving up the runners," said Frank.

"That's our cue, gentlemen and ladies, down we go," said Ian, and they all filed out the front door and then down the stairs to the hall.

"No special instructions," said Ian when everyone was ready and standing in the hall. "*Suerte* and don't fuck with the bulls, remember, it's their last run."

"*Suerte*," said Frank to Ian and Irina and the others.

"*Suerte, hermano,*" said Hector to Clive, and then the door was opened and they disappeared into the crowd.

"Look up," said Frank to Irina, as they walked towards the curve and Mercaderes, "look at all the people who've come to see you run."

"I'm famous," she told him, and Frank smiled and thought about last night and what had happened. Nacho had already left when Frank got up after no more than an hour of sleep, and everything that had transpired between the three of them was still somewhat fuzzy. Towards the end he had been very drunk and, perhaps, he couldn't remember correctly all the details but looking at Irina as she walked with him to the *curva*, he knew that he had been with her and had shared her with another man. Part of him, the jealous possessive part, said that what he had done was wrong, while the other part, the practical "can do" side of himself, said that that was probably the only way he'd ever have her.

"Very famous indeed," said Frank, as Irina looked up at the balconies above them.

Peter and Ilse walked to where Peter usually started his run, which was half way up Mercaderes at the intersection with Calle Chapitela. Clive had decided to take a chance with Ian on the far side of the curve, against the bull's eye boards. Ian said that he had never run it from there and had asked Clive to join him. Hector was starting about two meters from the curve, just ahead of where Frank and Irina were standing. He was stretching his arms into the air and bouncing on the balls of his feet, all the while feeling the space that he had chosen and the positive, spiritual energy that it afforded him. The Miura was one of the most noble and ancient breeding lines and he had always felt that it was a great honor to run with them. In his opinion, they were the true direct descendants of the Aurochs, by way of their stature, the size of their horns and their demeanor. They were untamed, regal and powerful, and they shook the earth itself when they ran.

Ian was wishing the three young Australians who were sharing the left side of the curve with him *suerte,* when he heard the first rocket go off. He waited for the second rocket and then looked at his watch and saw that hardly any time at all had passed between the two.

"This is going to be a fast one," he said to Clive, who looked back to see if he could see Peter and Ilse. They were standing where he'd seen them before and then he looked to the right side of the curve and saw Frank and Irina. They were surrounded and probably wouldn't get very far. Above them the noise of the thousands of people who were watching the *encierro* from the balconies grew louder as the herd made

163

its way up Santo Domingo, past the *Ayutamiento*, and finally to the beginning of Mercaderes.

"*Suerte!*" said Ian to Clive, and then he was off.

The herd was compact with two of the six hundred plus kilo bulls slamming into the boards. Of the three young Aussies two managed to get out of the way while the third tripped on the cobblestones just as one of the bulls was hurtling towards the curve. The bull stepped on his left leg and broke it but after that all it wanted to do was to rejoin the herd and the Aussie limped back to a point where a first aid team could pull him under the fence.

Clive started his run just after Ian and barely missed getting trapped against the curve with the young Australian. He ran straight ahead keeping to the left until he saw an opening that allowed him to sprint close to the lead bull. He was about to touch its flank when he was pushed by another runner and fell to the ground. Following close behind the lead bull, an even larger Miura saw Clive fall and tilting its huge head slightly to the left it came within two or three centimeters from impaling the Englishman's skull on its horn.

Hector was having another stellar *encierro*. He had chosen the right spot to begin with and everything flowed from that decision, in his opinion. The herd had accepted him at the edge of their space and he stayed with them almost to the end of Estafeta. It was a long run, and when he could no longer keep up with the bulls his heart was pounding and his lungs burned but he was a happy man. He had communed once more with his gods, with the Aurochs and the shamans, and had set in motion the next phase of his mania. And for that he was grateful.

Chapter 17

As Clive had predicted, Frank and Irina were surrounded by too many people and were unable to join the herd when it passed by. Still, Frank knew that just being there on the course, whether you were running or not, counted because shit could happen anywhere and what you might think was the safest place could in a matter of seconds become the deadliest. Luck was everything and you couldn't control that, in spite of whatever Hector had to say about finding one's ideal spot. Frank loved Hector like a brother but as far as he was concerned all this stuff about shamans and finding your spiritual "G-spot" was just Hector's San Diego version of Voodoo. If the bulls, for whatever reason, wanted to fuck with you then fuck with you they would.

Ian was waiting for Frank and Irina at Bar Fitero. He was sipping his cappuccino and ordered another two as they walked in.

"So, how did it go for you guys?" he asked.

"It didn't," said Irina.

"We couldn't move away from the curve and missed our sweet spot," said Frank.

"It happens, but if you want my advice," said Ian to Irina with a wink, "tomorrow you'd do well to run without him. He might be good with his cock when he hasn't had too much to drink, but he's bullocks with the bulls."

"You're one to talk," said Frank.

"Are you referring to the bulls or my life long search for the perfect cocktail?"

"Both."

"Well, at least I ran."

"And how did it go, maestro?"

"Let's watch and see," said Ian, looking up at the television above the bar.

"I can see Peter and Ilse," said Irina.

"There he goes," said Ian.

"What happened to Ilse?" said Frank.

"She fell," said Ian.

"Tough luck," said Frank.

"But looks like Peter didn't get that far either," said Irina.

"He tried to jump over some other guy, and that was the beginning of the end of his run," said Ian.

"Spanish television didn't even bother with us," said Irina.

"Well, of course not, my dear, you weren't moving," said Ian.

"Is that Clive?" asked Frank. "Nice sprint."

"And down he goes," said Irina.

"That was close," said Ian, "look at that second bull."

"Nasty," said Frank.

They all agreed that Hector won the prize for best run of the morning, even if Clive's fall and near fatal-encounter with one of the Miuras was hands down the most dramatic event.

After that they left the café and walked over to Txoko, where they found the rest of the crew.

"I'll get the drinks," said Ian, "you two run over there and find out what drugs Hector was taking to keep up with the herd."

"A triple dose of caffeine," said Frank.

"Amphetamines is more like it," said Ian.

"Amphetamines or his shamans," said Frank, and Ian laughed.

"Don't laugh."

"I'm not laughing," said Ian.

"It could be his secret weapon," said Frank.

"I'll be there in a sec," said Ian, still laughing.

"OK," said Frank, "and make mine a double."

"Yessir, Mr. Ardito."

For the media Clive's meeting with the Miuras was definitely a bigger draw than Hector's run. He was standing about ten feet away from the others and was surrounded by a group of print and TV journalists. They were asking him all the usual questions, was this his first time in Pamplona, what did he like about the *fiesta* and Spain, and, of course, what made him decide to take up bullfighting.

Hector was a better runner than Clive but Hector had been interviewed before, many times, perhaps too many times, and journalists always wanted something new.

"Just look at Clive," said Peter. "He's in his element. The TV cameras, the microphones."

"He's the star of the show," said Frank.

"Well, he earned it," said Hector.

"Not really, he fell down," said Peter.

"Yeah, but it was drama, and the TV gobbles up that shit," said Hector.

"By the way, I thought, we all thought, that your run was amazing," said Frank.

"Truly inspirational," said Irina.

"Hell, I was just in the right place at the right time. Pure luck," said Hector.

"I think pure talent has more to do with it than luck," said Frank.

"Well, three down and five more to go, and I honestly feel that the best is yet to come," said Hector.

"Here's to that," said Ian, as he joined the group and handed Frank and Irina their drinks.

"To the other *encierros*," said Peter, raising his glass.

"What I want to know," said Ian, interrupting the toast, "is what are you using to run like that?"

"What am I using? In what sense?"

"What's your drug of choice?"

"Nothing, just a croissant and your god awful coffee," said Hector with a smile. It made Ian and the others laugh, but what he had told them was only partially true. He wasn't taking any steroids or speed or erythropoietin (Lance Armstrong's pharmaceutical of choice), he had just stopped taking his daily dose of Lithium and that had made all the difference. The shaman who had spoken to him in his vision was right. His full emotional spectrum was now unfettered and he could explore feelings that his Lithium medication had declared out of bounds. Without Lithium the god-like sensations were returning. He felt

168

confident again, absolutely sure that any problem or obstacle could be overcome.

He had been taking the drug for five years since his diagnosis and this wasn't the first time that he'd stopped taking his meds, but it was the first time during the *fiesta* and he had to admit that he was excited. Not only because he was running better. The *fiesta* itself was the perfect environment for someone experiencing manic euphoria. It was the bipolar event *sans égal*, unrivalled and untamed, pagan and Catholic at the same time. In fact, Hector's behavior would pass largely unnoticed with most people thinking, oh he's just drunk and having a good time.

Indeed, the best was yet to come he thought. He felt virile, charming, super smart, sexy and ready to shine.

Later on, when Clive had finished his interviews and everyone was leaving Txoko Frank asked him if he would be going to the American party that afternoon.

"Absolutely, *hermano*, count on it," said Hector, and Frank laughed and walked away with Irina.

Chapter 18

The American party was always held in Plaza de San José, right next door to the Cathedral. It was a very quiet, secluded place, far from the *patxaran* zombies and the *peña* bands. The perfect location, Frank thought, to hold a get together for the *fiesta's* foreign regulars. There were trees and stone benches and plenty of room to gather and mingle, talk and drink. Frank had been coming to this party for years and being there meant that he had survived, almost, the first half of the *fiesta*, which would end at noon on the tenth of July, and that he had been sober enough to remember when and where the third of the trifecta of the expat parties was being held. It was a very good omen and yet another sign to convince him, if he ever needed more proof, that this was, without a doubt, one of the best *fiestas* he had ever had.

Of course, finding Irina was about as good as it gets. But finding her and figuring out just what it was that she wanted from him, if anything, were two completely different things. Yes, he had finally taken her to bed last night, together with Nacho, and while sleeping with her had been his goal from the moment he'd first set eyes on her at Café Iruña, there was that nagging sensation that he had never been in control, that it was Irina who was calling the shots and that he would have to abide by her rules for as long as it pleased her. Understanding that, effectively, she was the one on top and not him was not exactly a pleasant thought. It was a slap in the face to his male ego but he was persistent and would bide his time and see how events played themselves out. Literally anything could happen during the *fiesta,* so for now his plan was to behave himself, get thoroughly drunk, and observe.

"Just keep your cool and trust in the *fiesta,*" he said to himself, as he and Irina walked into the Plaza and saw Ian and Clive and the rest of the gang standing near the table with the drinks.

"Well, look who finally has arrived, the Italian stallion and his Slavic bride," said Ian, as he handed each of them a plastic cup of red wine.

"*Benvenidos,*" said Clive.

"Did we miss anything?" asked Frank.

"Not really, people are still wandering in," said Peter.

"Hi Peter, Clive," said Irina, giving each of them a kiss on the cheek.

"And me?" said Ian. "You kiss all the ugly ones and you forget about me?"

"Of course not," said Irina and she held out her hand so that he could kiss it.

"Ahhhh, Her Majesty, Princess Irina Romanova," joked Ian, making a very formal bow and then kissing her hand, both her cheeks and her lips.

"Frank, protect me from this kissing maniac," said Irina, as Ian continued to clown around.

"I could call his wife," suggested Frank.

"He's got a wife?" said Clive, looking surprised.

"Rumors that I've heard say that he does," said Frank.

"And fifty quid says that you're a liar," interjected Ian.

171

"Seriously, my sources say that he keeps her somewhere between Edinburgh and Glasgow and only lets her out on New Year's Day and their anniversary," said Frank.

"He's got a house up there, with a wife?" said Clive.

"I said nothing about a house," said Frank.

"More like a shoe then?"

"A gigantic shoe filled with fifteen kids," said Frank.

"Kids?" said Clive.

"Did I say fifteen?" asked Frank.

"You did," said Clive.

"Well, I meant to say fifty."

"Fifty fuckin' kids?" said Ian.

"Wee little ones," said Frank.

"And me wife takes care of them?"

"According to the rumors," said Frank.

"Ardito, you wanker, you need another drink," said Ian and he handed him his second plastic cup of wine.

"*Muchísimas gracias*," said Frank, who looked around and saw that many more people had arrived. There were all the expats, plus an unknown number of Spaniards who were either friends of expats or friends of friends. Hector was chatting up two American women, one of whom was a captain in the U.S. Army, while the other worked in Public Relations for a company in Austin. The women were very drunk and Hector himself was far from sober. They were all wearing fluorescent green Stetsons and were making the rounds of the party, with Hector introducing them either as his sisters or his fiancés.

172

"Ten euros says he shags the two of them," predicted Ian, as he waved the money in front of Frank's nose.

"I say he doesn't, but how would you ever find out?"

"Check their sheets in the morning," Ian told him.

"That would work," said Frank, "assuming they're virgins."

"The sheets don't lie," said Ian, a bit wobbly on his feet but absolutely on top of the situation when it came to not losing a drop of whatever he was drinking.

Frank looked over at the Cathedral and saw that Irina was standing next to Peter and Clive and a group of Swedes who were taking shots from a bottle of Absinthe in a game of "Last Man Standing". He was about to walk over there when Anton appeared out of nowhere and tapped him on the shoulder.

"Frank," he said, smiling his "it's *fiesta* and life is fucking amazing" smile.

"*Hombre*, where have you been?"

"Nowhere in particular, and everywhere at once, you could say."

"Of course. What's up?"

"Are you going to the *corrida* with Irrintzi?"

"Haven't seen Nacho, but I wouldn't mind going if we can get decent tickets."

"Ask Ian," Anton suggested.

"God no, enough of that nosebleed crap, I want to be able to see the matador and the bull for a change."

"So you've got some cash?"

173

"I can pay for the three of us, you, me and Irina, if the tickets are worth it."

"I'll find them for you," said Anton. "I know a few of the scalpers at the Arena."

"Is there anyone you don't know at this *fiesta*?"

"Doubt it," said Anton with a wink.

"Good," said Frank, "so let's see if Irina and her friends have room for two more."

"What are they drinking?"

"Absinthe."

"The Green Monster," said Anton.

"Anywhere from ninety to one hundred forty-eight proof. Serious drinking."

"More like suicidal," said Anton.

"Too much for you?"

"Not at all."

"Of course not," said Frank.

"We didn't invent it, but it is a Russian drink, in spirit at least."

"Hey Frank," said Peter, who was passing the bottle and the shot glass to the next in line.

"You mind if we join in?" said Frank.

"By all means," said Clive. "Our Swedish brothers came prepared, not one but two bottles of Absinthe."

"Two?" said Anton.

"And they want to finish them both. Isn't that right, guys?" said Clive, and the five Swedes smiled, waved and laughed.

"Awesomeness," said Frank.

"I was wondering when you were going to drag yourself away from Ian and join us," said Clive.

"What round are you up to," asked Frank.

"Fourth, no, third," said Peter, correcting himself.

"But who's counting," said Clive.

"Third," said Irina, who was now about to drink her fourth.

"Where did you find this stuff?" asked Frank.

"Here, in Spain, at a specialized shop in Madrid," said one of the Swedes.

Irina finished her shot, in one go, and then handed the bottle and the glass to Frank. He had a look at the bottle and saw that while it wasn't the highest proof it was somewhere above a hundred, which for him was a personal record. Not that it really mattered. The stuff was wickedly strong even at ninety proof, and he started pouring it into the glass with the Swedes encouraging him to fill it right to the top. Irina had filled it to the top and so he had no choice, they said. The honor of all men everywhere was at stake, they insisted, laughing and telling what he imagined to be off-color jokes in their own language.

"OK, right to the top it is," he said. "Do I have to finish it in one go?"

"No rules," said one of the Swedes. "You can finish it in one go or in two or however you want, just don't take forever, OK? We're all waiting our turn."

"Down the hatch," said Frank and he threw his head back and swallowed, the Absinthe burning his throat and warming his body all the way down to his stomach.

"My turn," said Anton, and he took the bottle and poured himself a shot.

"Are you sure you can handle this?" said Frank.

"You just wait, my friend, that was only your first glass. I intend to win this ridiculous game," said Anton.

"Sure, sure, but remember we're going to the *corrida*."

"I haven't forgot, but it's you I'm worried about. I might have to carry you there over my shoulder," he said, as he put the shot glass to his lips and drank deeply from the green monster.

"You're going to the *corrida*?" asked Clive.

"That's the plan," said Frank.

"Looking for tickets?"

"Yep."

"How many?"

"Three."

"Well, you're in luck, I happen to have exactly three extra tickets. I got them for some friends who were flying down from London, but their flight was cancelled and they're primo seats. You interested?"

"Where and how much?" said Frank.

"*Barrera*, second entrance. You're not going to find better than that."

"True, but how much?"

"You know, they were tickets I picked up two days ago for some colleagues of mine from work and money really wasn't a problem for these guys, if you know what I mean."

"OK, so how much of a loan will I have to get from my bank?"

"Loan?" said Clive, laughing. "Certainly you jest, brother, they're on the house."

"Come on, name your price."

"*Nada*," said Clive, "zilch, they're freebies."

"You're kidding?"

"*Hombre, somos hermanos, verdad?*"

"*Sí, claro.*"

"Well, you, Irina and Anton are my guests, oh, and Peter too, but then Peter already knew that."

"Wow, Clive, that's very…very, I don't really know what to say."

"How about thanks and drink up? It's my turn, Frank," said Clive, who took a sip from the shot glass before belting the rest of it down his throat and passing the bottle and the glass to Peter. "Another two rounds of this and then we have to get a move on if we still hope to get there and not end up crawling on our hands and knees."

By the time they left and had started to wander down through the crowds in the general direction of the bullring they were all drunk and hilariously doing their best to pretend that the Green Monster had no effect on them whatsoever. Clive spontaneously appointed himself the group's leader, not because he was any less drunk than the others, but because, having served as an officer in the Royal Air Force, he felt

177

that there was no one else better qualified to lead. Peter had also served, but he was too sloshed and happy to worry about the others or his military training. Irina was young and beautiful and knew that no matter what happened someone would be there to rescue her. Frank was neither young nor particularly handsome, but he knew that no matter how blitzed he became he would love Irina and that his job was simple: be the first man to save her before anyone else did. Anton was a psychiatrist and even as drunk as he was he knew that saving anyone was impossible but that counseling and therapy had a useful placebo effect.

At the entrance to the Plaza de Toros Clive counted heads to make sure that everyone was still with the group.

"OK, guys, I only see four here, there are five of us, correct?"

"You are joking?" said Peter.

"Cancel that, forgot to include myself," said Clive.

"I think we should avoid the Absinthe for a couple of days," said Frank.

"Not a bad idea," agreed Clive.

When they found their seats down by the *barrera* the ring was, of course, still empty and up in the stands where he usually sat the *peñas* had yet to arrive.

"What an incredible view," Frank said to Clive.

"You know, while I've been up there with the *peñas*, once, and once was enough, as an *aficionado* I can't understand how anyone would waste their money buying a *sol* ticket during the *fiesta*," said Clive.

"It can get hectic," agreed Frank.

"Chaotic and bedlam come to mind," said Clive.

"Well, I'm certainly not going to disagree with you on the atmosphere, but you have to admit you won't see that anywhere else in Spain."

"True, only here," said Clive.

"And even then, they aren't beating up on each other like they do in the UK or in Italy. Here there are no fans who are being literally crushed to death as they were, if you remember, in the European Cup final of 1985."

"We were both kids then," said Clive, "but you're right, this has nothing to do with hooliganism. Still, it is a distraction."

"José Tomás perhaps will never come here, but then he's always been a purist," said Frank.

"You've got something against purists, Frank?"

"No, but Pamplona is different. If anything, I say that only a truly great *torero* can concentrate on his art in the midst of all this chaos."

"Perhaps," said Clive.

"Focusing his strengths with Zen-like precision and tranquility."

"Frank," said Clive, laughing, "better to quit while you're ahead."

"Hey," said Peter, "excuse me if I'm interrupting my favorite philosophers but Anton and I are going on a beer run, you want some?"

"Sure," said Frank, handing him twenty euros.

"Make that two," said Clive.

179

"OK, with any luck at all we'll be back in time for the first bull."

"Thanks," said Clive, "I need something to wash that Absinthe out of my system."

"I don't think beer is going to do it, but it can't hurt," said Frank.

"Say, what are the two of you doing for dinner tonight?" said Clive.

"No plans," said Frank.

"Well, I've got reservations for five at the Europa, thanks to those London no-shows. Care to join me?"

"Just the three of us?" said Irina.

"And Peter and Anton if they want to come," said Clive.

"Why not?" said Frank.

"Great," said Clive.

"And here come the beers," said Frank.

"Just in time for the first bull," said Clive.

"There wasn't much of a line," said Peter, as he handed out the pints.

The bulls were enormous, of course. They were Miuras. But because they were so huge they were difficult to kill, especially for the matadors (all of them) under six feet. You couldn't go straight over the horns because of their size, and yet that is what you had to do. You faced the bull and you charged it and it charged you, and if all went well your sword didn't bounce off its spine and end up in the sand. The trick was to appear as if you were going over the horns but in fact only

180

a part of you, your right arm, was arching over its massive head. The rest of you sidestepped the bull.

This slight of hand didn't work with these bulls. The kills were a bloody mess and you could see that the matadors had much more a healthy fear of their huge horns. They were terrorized. One matador, desperate to kill his bull, which simply would not die after having been stabbed a dozen times in its neck muscle, had simply run up to the bull's right flank and stabbed it in its heart avoiding the horns altogether. The crowd and especially the *peñas* whistled loudly at the *torero's* lack of courage. Frank assumed that the last bull would be the same. It was the senior matador's turn and his *faena* was flawless, which given the nature of this particular group of Miuras was more than enough to make this a day that he wouldn't soon forget. But being an ambitious *torero* was just the beginning. He wanted to finish the afternoon in style and he wanted people to remember him.

The Miura stood in the exact center of the ring. Its shoulders were draped in its own blood and the six *banderillas* that had been put there by the matador's *banderilleros* to correct its tendency to use its right side more than its left. It was not moving, apart from its right hoof, which it stamped into the sand. It was waiting for the *torero* to make the first move. The spectators in the *sombra* seats maintained a respectful silence as the matador took aim with his sword, whereas the *peñas*, as usual, partied on.

When the matador began his final *estocada* there was no doubt in Frank's mind that he would succeed. He had never seen anything so perfect, so graceful and seemingly effortless. Then the bull twisted its

181

head slightly to the right and clipped the matador in his gut. When the matador hit the sand to the right of the bull he didn't move. There was blood all over his suit of lights and the enraged bull kept attacking the matador in his legs and his back until the animal was finally distracted and they were able to carry the *torero* out of the ring.

"Jesus," said Peter, " did you see that? That is one badass bull."

"Where are they taking him?" asked Irina.

"To the infirmary, and then by the looks of it to the hospital. He's definitely going to the hospital," said Clive.

"What are they going to do with the bull?" said Irina.

"What they always do," said Frank.

"It's up to the next most senior matador. It's his job," said Clive.

"To kill the bull?" said Irina.

"Yes," said Peter.

"Doesn't he get special points or an honorable mention or something for what he did?" Irina asked.

"Nope," said Frank, "that usually happens just before the matador is about to kill the bull, not after he's tried and the bull's gored him in his abdomen."

"The next most senior *torero* will do it, no question," said Clive.

"You know, while I'm sorry that the matador got hurt, I'm just as sorry for what's going to happen to that bull," said Irina, and neither Clive, nor Frank, or Peter had anything to say about that. What could they say? Fundamentally they knew that she was right. *Corrida* was, is and always would be unfair and a tragedy, no matter how you looked at

182

it. It was brutal and sensual and Spanish to the core, and yet every time a bull died Frank felt emotionally drained, cleansed in a weird way. It was something that he couldn't explain, a kind of closure, as if someone had forgiven him his sins and put an end temporarily to his pain.

Chapter 19

The thing that Frank remembered most about their dinner at the Europa was the red wine. Clive must have spent a fortune on those bottles, they were smooth beyond description and every time he refilled his glass he kept thinking about the story of those London bankers who spent the equivalent of twenty-two thousand U.S. dollars just on rare bottles of wine during their lunch break one day. Frank wasn't exactly poor but neither was he the kind of person who could afford to dish out for lunch what the average person might spend for a new car. Nor did the fact that Clive was paying for everything with thick wads of cash that he had stuffed into his pockets dispel Frank's idea that he might be spending the rest of the *fiesta* washing dishes in the Europa's kitchen if Clive's pockets weren't deep enough for the wine.

As it turned out, there was nothing to worry about. Clive had taken care of everything before hand and knew exactly how much the dinner, wines included, would cost him.

After the Europa they hit the clubs and the bars and drank and danced until half past two in the morning when Clive and Peter decided that if they wanted to do the run then they needed to get a few hours sleep. Frank agreed with them that sleep was not an option, even though Irina didn't feel tired at all and said to everyone that the night was still young. Anton, who apparently was an expert when it came to pushing the limits of insomnia, said that Irina could come with him.

"I'll bring her back to your place when she's had enough," he told Frank.

"Sure," he said, thinking that if worse came to worse he'd find her in one of the parks before the *encierro*, that or Nacho would find her first and take her back to an empty apartment that had been loaned to him for the occasion.

Just in case Anton didn't bring her back he gave her his spare key to the flat. She told him not to worry, kissed him and then disappeared into a crowd of people with Anton.

To be honest, Frank really needed to sleep. It was early morning on the tenth of July, the infamous halfway point of the *fiesta*, when even the hard core bar hoppers and partiers started to crash.

Just before he got to his apartment he heard someone calling his name and turned around to see Hector and his two fiancés.

"Frank, wait up!" said Hector.

"What's doin'?" said Frank. "I was just heading back to get some sleep before the run."

"Good man," said Hector. "You mind if we come with you? Can't seem to find my key to our place."

"Lost your key? Sure, no problem."

"Thanks, Frank."

"You're lucky that you and your lady friends ran into me, otherwise you might have had a problem finding somewhere where the three of you could crash."

"I know," said Hector, "it really is my lucky night."

"You can say that again," said Frank, looking at the Army captain and the PR executive.

"Hey Frank."

185

"Yes," he said, as he was opening the front door.

"I've got a car, and me and the fiancés are heading up to San Sebastian tomorrow morning after the run. It'd be really cool if you and Irina could join us."

"All five of us in your car, for a day at the seaside," said Frank, repeating what he had heard just to make sure that he was clear on what was being offered.

"Yessir, all five of us, in San Sebastian."

"Well, sure," said Frank, "why not?"

"*Hombre*," said Hector, "we're gonna have a great time!"

"Of course," said Frank, who was dead tired and who could think of nothing but getting in his bed and closing his eyes.

"You need a day off," said Hector, "we all do, and this is just what the doctor ordered."

For some reason hearing someone who was on a manic high, or fast approaching it, seriously talk to him about rest and doctor's orders, when he would probably spend the next three hours before the *encierro* fucking his fiancés until his nuts dropped off, sounded so preposterous he couldn't help but laugh.

"Sweet dreams," said Frank, as he left them in the living room and locked himself in his bedroom.

186

Chapter 20

Irina opened the door at ten past four in the morning and because it was very dark and she'd had a lot to drink in the bars with Anton she couldn't find the light switch and almost tripped over the naked bodies in the middle of the living room.

"Frank?" she said, but the man on the floor wasn't Frank, and she had no idea who the two women were. She walked over to their bedroom, tried opening the door, which wouldn't open, and then knocked softly to get Frank's attention. There was no answer.

She then put her ear to the door, waited and when she still couldn't hear anything she tiptoed as quietly as she could over to Hector's bedroom, took her clothes off and collapsed almost immediately into a deep sleep.

About an hour later and still quite inebriated and dreaming she half opened her eyes and everything that she saw was in her dream. It was a dream in which she had been travelling for some time to get to this room and where a muscular man who was naked and on his knees and straddling her hips was also a part of that dream. He was very handsome and polite, with jet-black hair and brown skin, and whispered into her ear that she had nothing to be afraid of and that he couldn't resist her and that everything would be all right. He said that he had been obsessed with her for some time now and apologized in advance for any inappropriate behavior on his part but that the moment had come for him to have sex with her. "Fair enough," was all she had to say, and the muscular man immediately began to rip off all of her

187

clothes in the classic heartthrob fashion of the soft-porn American Harlequin novels that her mother used to read after the fall of Communism.

A half an hour later Frank woke up, saw that Irina wasn't sleeping next to him and got dressed. On his way to the bathroom he passed by the open door to Hector's room and spotted her lying naked on the bed. He went in, closed the door behind him and sat next to her.

"It's Frank," he said, whispering into her ear.

"Yes," she said to him sleepily.

"Irina, it's me, Frank."

"Frank," she whispered to him, once her eyes were open and she could tell that it was no longer a dream, "who are those people?"

"Hector and his two fiancés."

"And what are they doing here?"

"Well, Hector is staying here, renting this apartment with me. I told you about that."

"Yes, you did, I think. And you know what, Frank, I think I had a dream about him earlier or at least someone who looked like him."

"Did you? That's interesting. Anyway, I ran into Hector and these two women on the way back to the apartment and he told me that he couldn't find his key and asked if I could let them in and, of course, I said yes."

"Of course."

"So, to make a long story short, Hector has offered to take us to San Sebastian in the morning, after the run, and I said "why not?"

188

"Oh, I like that idea," said Irina, still in part thinking about the dream and how very real it seemed.

"Great," said Frank.

"I've never been there before."

"You'll love it. It's really beautiful and when the sun's out and reflecting off the blue water and you're lying there on the hot sand you really can't ask for anything more."

"Except for maybe two ice cold cocktails for Mr. Frank Ardito and consort," said Irina.

"Exactly, plenty of those at the beach," said Frank. "So listen, I'm going to do the run and if you want to do it, too, then we go together. If not, we'll meet up at Bar Txoko afterwards, OK?"

"How about I meet you back here, I mean we're going to be wearing normal clothes, right? You'll be changing out of your whites, or no?" she asked and yawned.

"Good plan," said Frank, "and yes, normal clothes." At that point she closed her eyes and smiled and almost as soon as he put his arm around her she fell asleep.

At half past six Frank had a quick shower, got dressed, and when he came out of the bathroom Hector was standing there waiting for him. His fiancés were still on the floor, out cold.

"*Vámonos?*" asked Frank, and Hector gave him a thumbs up.

Once they were downstairs and outside Hector thanked Frank again for letting him in.

"Actually, you might want to thank the fiancés," said Frank. "Looks like you had quite a night."

189

"The Army captain runs marathons and she thought that she was in shape, but after an hour she had had enough."

"America's heroes just aren't what they used to be," said Frank, and they both laughed.

The streets in the center of Pamplona were as they always were just before the gates were closed and all the runners were corralled in front of the *Ayuntamiento*. Latecomers hurried to get to the City Hall in time, while those who were doing the *encierro* for the first time and who were lost were asking anyone they saw for directions to the starting line.

Looking up as they turned left onto Estafeta Frank could see that the balconies were already crowded.

"Have you ever been up there?" said Frank.

"Up where?"

"I mean, have you ever watched a run from up there," said Frank. "Just to get a different perspective?"

"Nope. Down here's the only perspective I'll ever need."

"Dumb question," said Frank.

"Kinda," said Hector, and they both laughed.

It was a beautiful day and when they got to Ian's apartment the view of the mountains in the morning was spectacular. The low white clouds and the light blue sky were a perfect frame for the dark green of the trees that ran from the base of the ridge to its peak.

"You should move here," said Hector, who was standing behind him, "with Irina, I mean."

"You think so?" said Frank.

190

"You could do worse," said Hector. "You could be happy here."

"I'll keep it in mind," said Frank.

"It's an option," said Hector.

"And a good one," said Frank, before he turned and left the balcony.

"All hail to the wanker in chief," said Ian, as Frank and Hector stepped back into the living room.

"You, guys want some of Ian's awful coffee?" asked Peter, who was standing in the kitchen with Clive.

"Well," said Ian, looking at Frank, "rumor has it that you're running some kind of house of the hotties up there in your flat."

"Says who?" asked Frank.

"Says our Chicano Casanova, that's who. Says that, a part from you two, there were three women in that flat last night."

"Is this true, Hector?" said Frank, feigning disbelief.

"I did ask you to let us in because I couldn't find my key, but I spent the night in the bathtub, as you know. I think the girls were on the couch or in my bedroom or something like that."

"Sounds pretty innocent to me," said Frank.

"I believe in Hector's innocence," said Clive.

"I second that," said Peter.

"The jury has spoken," said Clive, "a toast to the Chicano Casanova and his all night long innocence," and everyone, including Ian, said "hear, hear" and raised their coffee cups.

"OK," said Ian, "now that that's been settled will someone please turn on the telly and find out what bulls are running today."

191

"Torrestrella," said Clive, looking at the Diario de Navarra.

"And what do we know about Torrestrella?" asked Ian.

"They are not friendly," said Frank.

"Nor should they be kept as house pets," said Hector.

"Right," said Ian, "and how's the meat packing operation proceeding?"

"Everyone's been corralled and all the gates are shut," said Peter, who was standing in front of the TV.

"What time is it," said Ian.

"A quarter to eight," said Clive.

"Gentlemen," said Ian, "time to grab a sheet of newspaper and get our collective arses down there."

"Showtime," said Frank, as he rolled his baton and followed the others out the front door and down the stairs to the entrance hall.

"So, who's running from the curve," said Ian, when they were all lined up behind the front entrance.

"I'll be at the curve," said Hector.

"I'll be where I usually start, in Mercaderes," said Peter.

"What about the two of you," said Ian to Frank and Clive, "fancy running it from Telefónica?"

"I'm in," said Clive.

"A quick one through the tunnel, sure, why not?" said Frank.

"Good, time to go. *Suerte,* everyone!" said Ian and they filed out into the pack of runners. Hector and Peter turning right, while Frank, Ian and Clive walked to the end of Estafeta just before Telefónica. This was where the curve began that led down into the *callejón,* or tunnel, under the entrance to the bullring. It was the tail end of the course and while it wasn't as famous as the curve on Estafeta it was perhaps just as dangerous. The last recorded fatality during an *encierro* occurred in 2009 at Telefónica.

"About time for the first rocket," said Ian, looking at his watch.

"Telefónica," said Frank, "always full of surprises."

"There it is," said Ian, when he heard the boom.

"And there's the other one," said Frank.

"Won't be long," said Clive.

"Two, two and a half tops, they should be here," said Ian.

"Any *valientes*?" asked Frank.

"Can't see anything yet," said Clive.

"They should be where Peter is, more or less," said Ian.

"There, I can see the crowd getting pushed up Estafeta. People starting to panic, a few *valientes* and there," said Clive.

"Wait for it, gentlemen," said Ian, but Clive was already running. The first two bulls of the heard appeared suddenly out of the crowd, running with a steer through the curve, while the other four had fallen behind and were flipping and goring anyone who they could get their horns into on Estafeta.

Frank got about half way through the curve before he was knocked down by another runner. Ian was moving up the left side, trying to get to the two bulls before they reached the tunnel, but they were too fast. Out of breath, Ian saw Clive on the horns of the lead bull until the *toro bravo* sent him flying into the sand of the arena with a flick of its massive head.

When Frank got up from the cobblestones the four *sueltos* were still down at the other end of Estafeta. Bar Fitero wouldn't open their doors until all the bulls were safely in their pens behind the bullring. So he climbed over the wooden barrier and walked past the restaurant at Hotel Europa and then down the back alley that led to his café. When he got there the *sueltos* had been sorted out and the TV's above the bar were playing the re-runs of the *encierro*. He ordered a cappuccino and a croissant and watched the beginning of the run when the bulls together with the steers exited the holding pen at the beginning of Santo Domingo.

The problems began in Mercaderes. The first four bulls hit the curve more or less head on and lost contact with the herd and each other, while the two in the rear followed the steers to the bullring. As a result, when the first four got up again they did what all *sueltos* do, they began to stake out their own space, attacking anything that was within striking distance. One runner was gored in the back just below his right lung, while another was knocked to the ground but miraculously avoided injury, even though the bull tried repeatedly to stab him in his chest and abdomen.

Eventually the *Pastores*, professional bull handlers who wore green shirts and carried long cane polls, together with many of the more experienced runners, including Hector and Peter, were able to turn around the *sueltos* and drive them up Estafeta towards the Arena.

After watching the bulls run amok and listening to the commentary of the journalists on the bad luck of others of being in the wrong place at the wrong time, Frank thought, "What am I doing here?"

194

He had been coming to Pamplona for over a decade but only then, as he stood there looking up at the TV, did it occur to him how ironic it was that someone like him, with his troubled past and all his efforts to distance himself from the chaos that his father had represented, should so enthusiastically embrace the *encierro*. He was supposed to be different. That was the plan, and yet it seemed that the more you disliked someone or something, the more you kept telling yourself that you would never make the same mistakes, the more likely it was that you would repeat them. People got killed running with the bulls, it was dangerous and chaotic, and yet he ran, because he couldn't see himself not running and because it was beautiful.

"Screw it," he said, "there was no use in second-guessing what you loved," and he paid the bartender and left.

At Txoko Frank ordered an Absolut Bitch and joined Ian and the gang who were drinking and chatting as Clive answered a journalist's questions and was filmed by a television crew.

"We can't take this narcissist anywhere," said Ian, "not only is he an unworthy media magnet, but just look at him, look at that smile and those white teeth."

"You're just jealous," said Hector. "He did get thrown by a bull in the arena, if that isn't magnet worthy then I don't know what is."

"True," said Peter. "He's our hero for the day."

"Ardito, where the fuck were you?" said Ian.

"Got knocked down," said Frank.

"Any fall that you can walk away from is a good one," said Peter.

195

"And I saw that you and Hector were busy helping the *Pastores* turn those four *sueltos* around," said Frank.

"We did what we could," said Hector.

"Hey, so are we still on for San Sebastian?" asked Frank.

"Absolutely," said Hector. "You ready to go?"

"Pretty much, just need to change out of these. Don't know about the girls, though."

"Right," said Hector.

"Just add another hour for preparation time," said Frank.

"Ha! Sounds about right," said Peter.

"See you guys tonight," said Ian. "Have fun and get drunk for me."

"We'll try," said Hector.

***

The drive up to the ocean took them a little over an hour. Hector had rented a VW Golf and there was plenty of room in the back seat for Irina and one of the fiancés. The PR decided not to come. She couldn't remember anything about her night at Frank's, but once she had sobered up she said that she had other plans for the day. The Army captain was wearing white shorts and a tight fitting t-shirt with sandals, while Irina had chosen a light, knee-length red dress for the trip. Hector had changed into a tank top and shorts, while Frank had on a pair of loose off-white linen trousers tied with a rope belt and a blue t-shirt. They had a small duffel bag packed with beach towels, sun lotion and swim suits.

196

The drinks they would buy there because, as Hector liked to say, "Spain is one gigantic bar that's always open for business."

The city beach in San Sebastian wasn't packed when they arrived, but then it wasn't empty either.

"Hector, find us a place that's not too far from the water," said the captain.

"I'm looking," he said.

"Some place where we can all sit together," she insisted.

"Look," said Hector, "just pick a spot, here, there, wherever. There's tons of room."

"Over there," said Irina, pointing to a section of the beach that in her mind was closest to the island in the middle of the bay.

"Looks good to me," said Hector. "Sold, to the lady in red!"

"You going to swim to the island?" Frank asked.

"I might," said Irina, "if it gets too hot."

"The water's cold here," said Frank.

"No problem, where I come from it's warm in comparison."

As soon as they had set up the beach towels and had taken off their shorts, dresses, trousers and t-shirts Frank told Irina, "I think I'll pass on swimming."

"OK," said Irina.

Next to her Hector was helping the captain spread the sun cream lotion evenly on the hard to reach places. Irina watched them, and when she took the top of her bikini off Hector asked her if she needed a hand with her back.

"Sure," she said. His hands on her shoulders and spine felt very warm. She was lying on her stomach with her eyes closed and fantasizing about the dream where she had seen him. He covered everything from the nape of her neck down to the bottom of her spine and when his fingers accidentally slipped under her bikini and touched her where he shouldn't have she didn't say anything.

"OK, that about does it," he said. "I'm off for a swim. I'll be back in a bit."

"I'm coming with you," said the captain.

"And what about you, Irina?" said Hector.

"OK."

"A free drink for either of you if you can beat me to the island," said the captain.

"You're on," said Hector.

They ran into the surf and when it was deep enough they dove into an oncoming wave and started to swim. The captain took her challenge seriously and was already two lengths ahead of Hector. Irina, on the other hand, was anything but an avid swimmer. She had almost drowned once as a child and while she had agreed to go with them it was more due to her dream than any desire to swim in the cold Atlantic.

"How's it going?" Hector asked her when he had dropped back enough so that he was by her side.

"Good," she said.

"Listen, we can turn back if you want to. The captain is a bit of a fanatic about winning."

"No, I'm fine," she told him.

198

"Great," said Hector, and he stayed with her until they reached the island.

"Well, it looks like everyone's going to be paying for their own drinks today," said the captain, as she helped Irina up onto the dock.

"You beat us fair and square," said Hector.

"We can race back, if you want, double or nothing," said the captain.

"OK, but I win and you pay for everyone's drinks for the rest of the day," said Hector.

"Excluding Pamplona," said the captain.

"Including Pamplona."

"And if you lose?"

"Then the drinks are on me."

"For the whole day."

"For the whole fucking day," said Hector, holding out his hand.

"It's a deal," said the captain.

After a fifteen minute break standing on the dock Hector asked Irina if she was ready to swim back.

"Ready," she said, "but don't expect me to keep up with you guys."

"You'll be alright?" he asked her.

"I'm light," she told him, "I float. Don't worry."

"OK," said the captain, "see you all on the beach."

The three of them then dived off the dock, first the captain followed by Hector and finally Irina who was in no rush. When the captain emerged victorious on the beach Irina was still only half way there. She wasn't tired. She felt relaxed and was enjoying her swim and looking forward to a seafood lunch and cocktails.

"You lost?" said Irina when she saw Hector on the shore.

"Let's just say that I let her win."

"Ha! She beat you."

"Because I let her win."

"No, you didn't."

"Yes, I did," he told her, "because now I gotta pay for everyone's drinks."

"You sure do."

"And I feel like celebrating today. I want to get everyone drunk on my money."

"Well, we were going to do that anyway, to get drunk that is," said Frank, who had joined the group.

"Whether you paid for the drinks or not," added Irina.

"Think what you want," said Hector, "I'm just happy that the tab's gonna be on me."

"You better believe it," said the captain, who suddenly jumped on him, wrapping her arms around his shoulders and her legs around his hips.

"I believe it," said Hector, as the captain kept kissing him. "Really, I believe it."

"Time to get back to the party or do we have lunch first?" said Frank.

"Lunch!" said Irina.

"OK, I was just kidding. I know of a good place."

"Quiet and yet elegant?" Irina asked.

"Yes," he promised, and Frank took them to a small restaurant with a bar near the ocean where the seafood was fantastic and the wine and the cocktails even better. After many courses and desserts and bottles of rosé it was close to six in the afternoon when they finally drove back to Pamplona.

Chapter 21

After Hector parked the Golf in the underground garage of Plaza Castillo everyone agreed to meet at eleven in Calle Labrit at the Txirrintxa. But when eleven came and went Frank and Irina had showed up along with Hector, but the captain was nowhere to be seen.

"Do you think she's coming?" asked Frank, as the three of them stood outside the bar with their Gin and tonics.

"Doubt it," said Hector, "she told me she was married and that she was determined to make the most of this *fiesta*."

"Oh well, if that's the case…" said Irina.

"Then you're a free man," said Frank.

"Another night, another lover," Irina added.

"But then if she can do it, so can you," said Frank.

"It won't take her long to find someone new," said Hector.

"Forget her," said Frank, raising his drink for a toast.

"Yeah, forget her," said Irina, lifting her Gin and tonic up to Frank's.

"Thanks, guys," said Hector.

"What are friends for?" said Frank.

"I've got an idea," said Irina.

"Shoot," said Hector.

"Let's have another drink, something different, something strong, and then let's find a locale where we can dance."

"*Excelente*," said Hector. "What do you think, Frank?"

"Absolutely, one more drink then we're outta here."

"Three Vodka tonics," shouted Hector to one of the barmen, "and don't go easy on the vodka, OK?"

"*Vale*," said the barman, and after a few minutes they had their drinks.

"Wow, this is strong," said Irina.

"Strong even for a Russian, must be a killer drink," said Hector.

"Taste it, if you don't believe me," she said.

"It is," agreed Frank. "Great drinks," he said to the barman.

"Well, the drinks are still on me, so I pay," said Hector.

"What do you mean *still on you*?" said Irina.

"You remember, I lost the race," said Hector.

"Yeah, but she's not here and I doubt if any of us will ever see her again, so forget it," said Frank.

"OK, but this round's on me," said Hector.

"And I've got the next one," said Frank.

The disco that they went to was just down the road. At midnight it was packed and overflowing to the point where there were people dancing out on the street.

"Now this is what I call a proper party," said Hector into Irina's ear so that she could hear him with all the noise. Frank had gone inside to the bar to get some more Vodka tonics, but Hector thought that he wouldn't need another drink and that, even if he did continue to drink, it wouldn't alter in any way the sensation he had of his power and the ability to do whatever came to mind. His manic high had returned with a vengeance. The soothing atmosphere of a morning spent by the sea with the sound of waves crashing against the beach and drinks in the afternoon had perhaps temporarily weakened his power, but the bacchanalia of the *fiesta* had revived it and he knew that this time he would ride it as far as it would take him. He had no need for medication nor was it his desire to be cured, he just wanted to be himself.

"Dance with me," said Irina, and Hector pulled her close so that she could feel how hard he was. There was barely any room to move in the crowd and Hector slipped his hands into her shorts.

"I've been wanting this since San Sebastian," he told her.

"Me too," she said, and he kissed her.

When Frank returned with the drinks the three of them danced together and whenever Frank went back to the bar Hector and Irina would pick up wherever they had left off kissing and touching each other.

Finally, some time after three in the morning, when Frank was about to return to the bar Hector said, "Speaking of drinks, do you think you could get us a round of tequila shots?"

"Just one round," said Irina, "why not four?"

"*Mamma mia*, where did you find this woman, Frank? Cast iron stomach and nerves of steel."

"At Café Iruña, where all good women can be found," said Frank, giving Irina a kiss. He then went off to the bar to get the drinks. When he came back he was carrying an open bottle of tequila with three shot glasses, but Hector and Irina had disappeared.

Chapter 22

As soon as Frank went to get the tequila Hector and Irina bolted out the front door of the discotheque and kept running until they were out of breath and laughing in front of Bar Txoko.

"That was some escape," said Hector.

"If it had been up to me, I would have left much earlier," said Irina, her face still flushed from their mad dash.

"Do you want something else to drink?"

"A Gin and tonic, please," she said.

"Coming up," he told her and he walked over to the take-away window and ordered one for her and for himself.

When he got back with the drinks he saw that Irina was chatting and laughing with a young woman who looked to be about the same age as she was. She had light brown hair and judging from her accent Hector guessed that she might be from Argentina or Chile. She had been looking for her group of friends when she'd bumped into Irina. She said her name was Clara and after Hector got her a refill on the mojito she was drinking they asked her if she wanted to join them for a bit of dancing at the Basque bars.

"And where are the Basque bars?" she asked.

"Not too far from here," said Irina.

"And what's so special about them?"

"Everything!" exclaimed Irina.

"OK, if you say so, why not?"

As they strolled across the Plaza Castillo, Hector walked a few steps behind Irina and Clara. From this vantage point he could watch the way they moved and imagine himself with one or the other or both of them in bed. Honestly, he didn't think that there would be a threesome. Not tonight, at any rate. He had just had one yesterday and two in a row was perhaps too much good luck for anyone, even for someone as fortunate with women as he was. Still, there was no denying that threesomes were a treat and if that was what the gods had in mind for him tonight then so be it.

"Where are you from?" he asked Clara, as they turned left on Mercaderes.

"Argentina."

"Buenas Aires?"

"No, I don't live on the coast."

"Where then?"

"Cordoba. In the center of the country."

"Never been there," he said.

"And where are you from?" she asked him.

"San Diego."

"So you're an American."

"Born and raised."

"But you don't look like one."

"No?"

"No, you look more Mexican than American."

"My parents were migrant farmers. They moved to California because that was where the work was."

"So that's how you speak perfect English."

"Pretty much."

"And he's a boxer, too," said Irina when they were in front of the Basque bar that she had chosen.

"Oh really?" said Clara, suddenly noticing Hector's athletic body.

"Really," said Hector, smiling at both Irina and Clara.

"Feel his muscles, if you don't believe me," Irina joked.

"I believe you," said Clara.

"Touch him anywhere," said Irina, "he's rock solid."

"Punch me in the stomach," said Hector.

"Here?" she asked, indicating more or less where his bellybutton was.

"Sure," he told her, and she punched him as hard as she could, but instead of hurting him she hurt her fist.

"Ouch!" she shouted.

"You see what I mean?" said Irina.

"I do," admitted Clara, "solid as a rock."

"Do you want another refill on that mojito?" Hector asked Clara, as they entered the Basque bar.

"Yes, thank you, *muchas gracias.* That would be lovely."

"You know what I find sexy about you?" whispered Irina into Hector's ear, as they all waited for the bartender to make Clara's mojito.

"No, tell me," said Hector.

"You are not at all like Frank."

"*Mi hermano*? How so?"

"Well, for starters, you flirt with everyone and yet you belong to no one."

"And Frank?" said Hector.

"He flirts with no one and thinks that I belong to him."

"You've been treating him like shit," said Hector, "you know that, don't you?"

"I have, but he doesn't own me and neither do you, but misbehave yourself and you can have me and her tonight, if that's what you want."

"Mighty generous of you," said Hector, with more than just a touch of sarcasm in his voice.

"I know what you want."

"I think you do," he said, as the bartender handed him the mojito, which he gave to Clara.

"Time to dance!" said Irina and she disappeared into the mob of people on the dance floor.

Hector ordered a mojito for himself and another one for Irina, as he stood at the bar with Clara.

"She'll be back soon enough," said Hector and in fact when the bartender gave him the other two drinks she showed up to ask them if they were going to dance.

"Gotcha a mojito, care to join us?"

"No, I'm going to dance, you keep an eye on it for me," and she darted off into the crowd.

"She's pretty intense," said Clara.

"She is," Hector agreed.

"How long have the two of you been together?"

"We aren't," said Hector, "we're just friends."

"I see."

"And what about you? Are you together with anyone?"

"Well, I'm here with the two of you tonight. How's that?" she asked, pinching him in the ass.

"Sounds good. What do you say we join her?"

"Lead the way," said Clara, holding her mojito in one hand and Irina's in the other.

As usual, she was in the middle of the crowd of dancers and doing her own thing, oblivious to anyone and anything but the music. Clara whispered something into her ear and Irina turned and kissed her on the lips.

"Here's your drink," said Clara, loud enough this time so that Hector could hear her.

They stayed there for a while, dancing and drinking and making out, and when they were all thoroughly drunk they walked back to the apartment, got naked and locked the front door.

Chapter 23

He looked for them everywhere. At first thinking that maybe she wasn't feeling well. That perhaps the alcohol and fatigue had finally gotten to her and that Hector had taken her outside for a bit of fresh air. But they weren't outside the club and he expanded his search to a number of other bars where he thought they might have gone. Of course, at that point he wasn't terribly optimistic and knew that his chances of casually running into either of them were next to zero. He didn't even bother checking at their apartment. He thought that if that was where they had gone then good riddance to her. He spent the rest of the night in the Basque bars, drinking and dancing and chatting up other women.

Some time before six he woke up on a park bench in the arms of a woman who he'd met in one of the bars. She had a name but he couldn't remember it, nor could he remember how exactly they had ended up there or what, if anything, they had done together.

His first thought, as he stood up and looked down at her, still soundly asleep on the bench was of Irina and where she and Hector had spent the night. Naturally, Frank imagined finding the two of them back in the apartment. He would climb up to the fourth floor where he would open the front door with his key only to see Hector sitting on the couch fully dressed and telling him in a calm, happy voice: "Hey Frank, me and your honeybunch had one hell of a time fucking last night, but now we gotta get a move on, the *encierro* beckons. You coming?" It was the sort of thing his old man would say when he was manic, messing around with Frank's ego and then perhaps suggesting that they go get a coffee, a bite to eat or catch a movie together.

But Hector was not his father. He was a good friend and someone who he thought he could trust. But then, considering where they were, could he even think of this as a betrayal of his trust? This was *fiesta*, after all, Pamplona, and crazy things happened here all the time. Wild bordering on insane was just one of the *hors d'oeuvres* of this bacchanalian feast. You needed to expect the unexpected here, he reminded himself and if the girl you were with spent the night with some other guy then maybe that wasn't such a horrible thing. Frank wasn't married to her or anything like that, in fact he barely knew Irina. Besides, if he still wanted her, Frank was sure that Hector would find another woman before the day was over. He wasn't counting on it, but you never knew, he might run into her again.

Walking down Estafeta near the curve Frank was thinking about *malas mujeres*, the *fiesta* and Ian's horrible coffee when someone following him tapped him on the shoulder.

"*Hombre*," said Hector, wearing the same clothes he'd had on at the club, "where did you disappear to last night?"

"No, I didn't disappear, Hector, you and Irina did."

"Frank, we looked for you everywhere, I swear."

"Yeah, right."

"I mean it, one minute you were getting drinks and then the next we couldn't find you."

"Tell me about it."

"Honestly," said Hector, with a serious look on his face.

"And so you took her back to our place?" said Frank.

"Where else?"

"And you fucked her, of course."

"Well, she wanted it. What was I going to do, refuse?"

"You tell me."

"Hey Frank, you can't blame me this time."

"How's that?"

"I can't help it, man, lately I've been obsessed with pussy. I mean, I don't know how many girls I've fucked in the last month, really it's not my fault."

Frank saw the elation mixed with confusion in his eyes and realized that he was telling the truth. Hector hadn't taken his meds and like anyone who was bipolar, once he had convinced himself that he didn't need the Lithium anymore there would be no stopping the mania until he crashed.

"So it's pussy this time," said Frank, marveling at his friend's ability to take a heavy night of non-stop partying, alcohol and fornication with absolutely no visible side effects. The man was a sexual cyborg with a power plant that would never die, which was not at all how Frank was feeling right then. He was tired after a night out in the open and needed a coffee badly.

Hector then confessed as they stood in front of Ian's building that he had had a great night and that Irina was incredible but that he had no real interest in her.

"Don't get me wrong, she's a hell of a woman, but she's your woman, Frank, if you still want her, not mine. If anything, what happened last night is what I might call a natural strengthening of the bond between you and me, as brothers. You know what I mean?"

"Sure," he said. "Why not?"

"Frank, let me be straight with you, your generosity is something that I will never forget."

"Generosity? What are you going on about?" asked Frank, laughing at his friend's choice of words.

"The fact that you could share with me a woman who in my humble opinion stands a good chance of becoming the love of your life is tremendous. *Hermano,* there are simply no other words to describe what I experienced."

"I didn't share anything with you," said Frank.

"No, *hermano*, it was love, brotherly love," Hector insisted.

"Look, Hector, you're making me laugh. You fucked Irina and there isn't anything I can do about that. However, you are still my brother and if you needed her then you needed her. What else can I tell you?" said Frank.

"Well, if you ask me, she isn't the person you think she is."

"No?"

"Nah, you're way too good for her."

"You think?"

"I know, brother, believe me, I know."

"No, she's better than that."

"I wish I was wrong, Frank, but I'm not this time. She uses men, and she'll spit you out just as soon as she's had enough."

"I still don't believe you."

"I know what you want, Frank. Ideally it's what we'd all like, but that kind of loyalty you just don't find anymore. These days they all want to conquer the world, so you got to get it when you can and be grateful for whatever crumbs they throw in your direction."

"Truth," said Frank.

"You know I wouldn't lie to you about that," said Hector and he gave his friend a hug and pressed Ian's number on the intercom.

Up in the apartment Frank listened to Ian's usual assortment of crude jokes and then when it was time they all marched down the stairs to join the rest of the runners on Estafeta.

Frank followed Hector because he knew that no matter how well the others ran Hector always had a plan and that it usually ended with him running on the horns of a *toro bravo*.

"Did I ever tell you that every shaman has to find his own space," Hector said when they stopped about half way up Estafeta. "This is the spot where you feel your own energies best. Your space is perhaps somewhere else, Frank. But only you would know. Still, if you feel strong here we can run together."

"I feel great," said Frank, with just a touch of irony in his voice, thinking why the hell shouldn't he feel that way when it seemed like everyone he knew was going to bed with Irina.

Hector looked at his watch and at eight the rockets punctually exploded over the *Casco Viejo*. Then when the herd came thundering up Estafeta Frank couldn't keep up with Hector nor was he as good at dodging obstacles. Just before Telefónica he tripped over another runner who had slipped on the cobblestones.

Later at Bar Fitero he watched the video of the *encierro* and saw Hector running on the horns of the lead bull through the tunnel and out into the arena. He looked strong and calm and if Frank didn't know better he would have sworn that the bulls had accepted him as one of their own.

Chapter 24

When Frank went back to the apartment after meeting up with the guys at Txoko Irina was still sleeping in Hector's room. It was going to be another hot day and she was lying naked on top of the sheets with the fan turned on full blast. For a moment he just stood there at the door and looked at her, but then he quickly took off all his clothes. At first he caressed her and gently kissed her until she pulled him closer and whispered into his ear that she loved him and that she had felt this way for some time now. She had yet to open her eyes and he wasn't at all sure that she knew that it was Frank and not Hector. Nor could he be sure that what she was telling him wasn't coming directly from some dream that she was having. But did it really matter, he asked himself as he made love to her? He and Hector had always shared everything over the years. But who did Irina belong to? Who did she want? Was Hector right about Irina and Frank was just being a fool? Who could say.

Afterwards, when they had finished and he was lying next to her and was certain that she was awake, he asked her why she had left him the night before.

"It's kinda obvious, isn't it?"

"I guess so, but I just wanted to hear you say it," Frank told her.

"I wanted Hector."

"That I knew."

"I wanted him from back there on the beach, no, even before San Sebastian."

"I kind of figured that."

"But I wanted him alone, Frank, not with you or Nacho, just Hector."

"And now that you've been alone with him what's your verdict?"

"That's a secret."

"He says that you're dynamite in bed, by the way."

"What! When did he tell you that?"

"This morning, before the *encierro*."

"I specifically told him not to talk about it."

"As if he wouldn't. We're pretty close. Really you should be thinking of us as identical twins, although we're not. We're not related, not at all. We had different mothers, fathers. We went to different schools, grew up in different towns. We don't even look alike, he's a Chicano and I'm an Italian-American. He's brown and I'm not. We have absolutely nothing in common but we're brothers just the same, and it's always been that way from the day we met."

"I know that," she told him.

"Oh yeah?"

"Yes, because he told me everything about you, last night."

"That must have been quite the conversation."

"It was," she told him, "he says that you're one of the few people he trusts."

"Doesn't surprise me."

"Says you've always protected him."

"Hector is a big guy, he doesn't need me for that."

"Says you've always been there to pick up the pieces."

"Well, that's something else."

"True, but he depends on you," said Irina, as Frank stared up at the ceiling.

"OK, so I pick up the pieces. Have you also been enlisted in this emergency aid program of his?" asked Frank.

"Well, I don't know if this is going to help him, but he asked me if I'd be willing to take part in a threesome with him and another woman."

"Well, you are the expert in threesomes."

"Ha!"

"And what did you say?"

"Sure, why not?" she told Frank, omitting the fact that she'd already had a threesome with Hector.

Frank thought it was curious, to say the least, that here was someone who not too long before had told him that she loved him and now she was talking about threesomes with another woman and his best friend. Logistically perhaps there was nothing that excluded the possibility of her being in love with Frank and wanting at the same time to take part in a *ménage a trois*. She had done it before and Frank figured that all anyone had to do was get drunk enough and any moral hurdles encountered during the *fiesta* were a piece of cake. Emotionally, however, there was something about it that didn't quite sit well with him. Yet, perhaps that was what the *fiesta* was all about, the more bottles of Rioja, pints of beer and rounds of tequila you had the more you were able to shut out the emotional filters and give free reign to

218

your inner sinner. And if at the end of those nine days you were neither changed nor damaged but you had had your fun, well, that was what counted. The *fiesta* wasn't going to cure you of anything. It was just an aspirin you took at the beginning of July to help ease the pain and boredom of modern living.

***

Because she was hungry Frank took Irina out to breakfast where they usually ate at the café on Calle San Agustín with the long tables on either side of the street. There they met up with some of the other runners that Frank knew, mostly locals, all of them speaking at the same time, cracking jokes and technically critiquing Hector's run. They were saying things like "he honored the *encierro*" and "that was how you were supposed to do it" and "finally, an American who understands something of our culture". Of course, there were others who called him a narcissist and a show boater, but for the most part they were singing his praises.

"What are they going on about?" Irina asked, as she drank some of her coffee, and then took a sip from the glass filled with red wine.

"About your other lover," said Frank.

"Which one?"

"Ah, that's right, we're up to three now, that I know of. The Chicano boxer."

"Hector!"

"He made quite an impression on everyone in this morning's run."

"Well, you want to know something?"

"What?"

"He called me his secret weapon and said that by taking me many times he was enhancing his powers of perception and that whatever he did today would be because of me."

"Well, your magic seems to have worked, my dear," said Frank, who could barely keep himself from laughing.

Over the years he had heard many of Hector's lines to women, but this one was over the top. With this one he hit the ball right out of the park. Frank could just imagine Hector explaining it to Irina, saying that because he was fucking her he could now literally feel the future and see clearly where his center of power lay, no matter what position of the Kama Sutra they were doing it in.

"Frank, he is unlike any man I have ever met before," said Irina, squeezing Frank's hand as he was about to fork another piece of *txistorra* into his mouth.

"You're right about that one," said Frank, "couldn't agree with you more."

After breakfast they walked over to the bullring and then over to the other side of town where they watched the ducks and the peacocks at the Parque de la Taconera. It was a relatively quiet place outside of the *fiesta* with flowers and long, tree-lined paths and benches where they could sit and kiss. As he walked with Irina through the park Frank thought that this was as close to perfection as he could imagine or might ever have. He was somewhat at peace with himself for a change and in love with her, even if she wasn't his nor in all probability would she ever be. It didn't matter anymore. Something had changed in him and he had let her go only to discover that he was closer to her now than when he had yet to give up any pretense of possessing her.

When they finished their stroll through the park and the sun had risen high in the sky they wandered back to Plaza Castillo where they saw Hector sitting at a table in Windsor Bar with a young Latina from Mexico. Her name was Ana and she was the other woman that he had found for his second threesome with Irina.

"What are you two having?" asked Hector, as Frank and Irina sat down at his table.

"Beers, I guess," said Frank, "I think we're also going to order two plates of *pulpo a la Gallega*."

"Well how about we make that four," said Hector, "I'm treating."

"Thanks, man!" said Frank. "The drinks are on me then."

Now that they had all decided on what to eat, Frank and Irina introduced themselves to Ana, who didn't look to be a day over twenty. She was from Merida on the Yucatan peninsula and had the same dark hair and eyes that Hector had but a much lighter complexion. She was doing the Camino de Santiago and had taken a break for a few days to experience the *fiesta* for the first time. Having been raised a Catholic the thought of refreshing her spirituality on the Camino appealed to her but then so did the idea of awakening her inner sinner during the *fiesta*. She had met Hector after the *encierro* and they had hit it off right from

221

the moment they saw each other. Likewise, Irina was very impressed with Ana. She had a kind of fetish for Latinos and South Americans in general and as the lunch progressed and the beers were replaced by Gin and tonics and stronger cocktails she began to flirt both with Hector and Ana.

While Frank still wasn't ready to call Irina a bisexual, it was clear that she was anything but immune to the charms of a pretty woman. Her behavior that afternoon reminded him of the day when she and Marcy had flirted at the Vodka Party, touching and kissing each other while laughing and joking with everyone else.

When Clive showed up he found a chair and positioned it so that it was between Ana and Irina. He impressed Ana with his knowledge of Mexican novelists and spoke to her exclusively in Spanish, which annoyed Irina, because her Spanish was not that good. She didn't like being excluded from the conversation and started pinching Clive around his waist and even lower.

"Behave yourself, Irina, or I will be forced to resort to 'drastic' measures," he said.

"You wouldn't," she dared him.

"You've been warned," he told her, and she pinched him again on the inside of his left thigh.

"There!" he said, pinching her back just below her right breast.

"Ouch!" she said. "That hurt!"

"I told you."

"Now kiss it and make it better," she said, lifting her shirt and pointing to where he had touched her.

"Here?" he asked, licking the spot she had indicated.

"No," she said and pointed to her breast.

"Well, I'm afraid I can't do that here, you'll have to wait," he told her.

"Not fair, it still hurts."

"Later," he said, "I promise." And she kissed him on the lips. At that point Clive said that he was going to the bar and asked if anyone needed another drink.

"Irina, Ana? You ladies up for another of whatever it is you're drinking?"

"I'm good," said Ana.

"No, you're not," said Irina, "two Bloody Mary's, Clive."

"OK, and what will the two gentlemen be having? Frank, Hector?"

"Gin and tonic for me," said Hector.

"A Rum Collins for me," said Frank.

"Excellent, two Bloody Mary's, a Rum Collins and a Gin and tonic. Coming right up," he said and disappeared into the crowd at the entrance to the bar.

"Your friend is quite the gentleman," said Ana, leaning across the table so that Frank could hear her.

"He is," Frank agreed, "*y tambien muy mujeriego* (and also very much a ladies man)."

"*Claro,*" she said, "but that's good and very much in keeping with the spirit here."

223

Frank smiled, he had a feeling that it was going to be an exceptionally interesting afternoon and evening. Where he was sitting he had a good view of the Plaza and as the hours passed he watched people gather around the stage where a DJ led a group in a sort of Salsa line dance, only to see them dissipate when the sun began to set and another group took over the center of the Plaza with their traditional Basque folk music and dancing. Everyone who passed by was encouraged to join in, and at one point he was sure that he could see Peter and Ilse trying to imitate the movements of the dancers, even though they were both visibly sloshed.

With darkness the crowds increased along with the noise and the excitement that he could feel in the Plaza. At half past ten in the evening Clive was still sitting at their table, and Frank thought that this would be the group that would boldly go where none of their morals could follow.

"Shall we do a little Basque bar hopping?" asked Hector.

"Bit early for that, don't you think?" said Frank.

"Not at all," said Hector.

"I want to dance!" said Irina.

"Me too," said Ana.

"Well, we could go to the Basque bars or the clubs," said Clive.

"Should we flip a coin?" asked Frank.

"A show of hands, please," said Hector, "all those in favor of the clubs raise your hand." And Frank was the only one to raise his hand.

"The Basque bars have it," said Hector, who waved down a waiter so that he could pay the tab.

"I'll get it," said Frank.

"*Hombre,* we've been sitting here hours," said Hector, trying to dissuade him.

"*No te preocupes* (don't worry)," Frank told him, "I got this."

"Hey, thanks, Frank."

"He's paying for everything?" asked Clive.

"Yep," said Frank.

"OK, then the rest of the night is on us, brother," said Hector.

"*Gracias,*" said Frank and when he came back from paying the bartender and everyone else who had to pee had used the toilets the five of them set off arm in arm for the Basque bars.

Chapter 25

What Frank remembered most about the bars was how Irina danced. She danced as if there were no tomorrow, with such abandon and intensity that all those who saw her couldn't help but feel her energy. She danced with men and with women and many of them afterwards felt the need to embrace or to kiss her and she didn't seem to mind. Of course, there was always someone keeping an eye on her, someone from their group. They were being protective, and Frank thought that it was true that her freedom to be the woman she felt she was and to do the things that she needed to do at the *fiesta* was guaranteed by the protection of her *cuadrilla* or group. No one was going to do her any harm, and if any man even so much as tried he would soon be made to forever regret his inopportune decision.

To celebrate the fact that Irina and Ana were now a part of the *cuadrilla* Clive bought a bottle of vodka and a bottle of tequila at a twenty-four hour convenience store. However, when the five of them stumbled into Frank's apartment a few hours before sunrise the real surprise and celebratory gift was Hector's small clear plastic bag filled with marijuana, rolling paper and two joints.

"Where did you get that?" asked Clive.

"I've got my contacts, bro," said Hector.

"*Perfecto*," said Ana, as Hector handed her one of the joints.

"Light that baby up," said Hector, just before Ana took a toke and passed the joint to Irina.

"A great way to end the night," said Frank.

"What do you mean, end the night, the night is still young!" said Irina, and Frank laughed.

Soon everyone else was chatting and laughing at even the stupidest things. Clive said that they should be dancing and Hector said, "OK, show us what you got."

"I need a partner," said Clive.

"No, by yourself," said Hector, "and any contestant has to dance what we decide."

"Oh, come on this is ridiculous. Irina, dance with me."

"Only if you kiss my boob," she said, lifting her shirt off, "you promised."

"I did no such thing," said Clive, laughing, "I just told you that I couldn't do it there at the bar."

"Well, we're not at the bar, what are you waiting for?" she said, trying to look angry but laughing because of the marijuana.

"OK, OK, you convinced me," and he walked over to where she was and kissed her on the nipple.

"Not enough," said Irina.

"What do you mean?" asked Clive. "That was my promise, one nipple."

"Not so fast, big guy, if you really want me to dance with you then you gotta pay the price," she told him, laughing.

"OK, you win," he said and kissed her other breast. The rest of the group clapped their hands and cheered, while Hector whipped out his phone and immortalized the moment for Instagram. After that Frank remembered that the pace of events quickened noticeably. Irina kissed

227

Clive. Hector kissed Ana who kissed Frank who kissed Irina who took her skirt off with Clive's help. Everyone was touching everyone and dancing and drinking, laughing and smoking Hector's weed. Desires were expressed, inflamed and quenched, and everything that they did in that room and in the other rooms of that apartment was a secret of the *cuadrilla*.

They partied until they fell asleep and when they finally began to open their eyes again at one in the afternoon the *encierro* was already ancient history for those who had run it. Another day at the *fiesta* had begun with more parties, chance encounters and verities revealed about love, life, death and the human condition. The Taurine gods looked down on the bacchanalia that they had wrought and were pleased. All was as it should be and had been since the beginning of human history when those first few artists who had understood everything began to dream in their Paleolithic caves.

Chapter 26

That afternoon the five of them had lunch at Casa Otano and after that they bar hopped until it was time to go to the *corrida*. Clive got everyone tickets in the *palco*, close to where the president of the jury sat. There Hector was finally able to get a good look at the bulls that he had missed in the morning and that had gored two runners near Telefónica.

In the evening they had *pinchos* and cocktails at various bars and then went dancing when Irina said that it was time to dance. They returned to the apartment late but Hector made sure this time to set the alarm. He wasn't going to miss another *encierro* and at six o'clock he took a shower and then shook both Frank and Clive, saying that if they wanted to run today now was the time to get up.

Outside the sky was clear although it had rained during the night and the three of them walked down the wet cobblestones of Calle del Carmen until they got to Estafeta and turned left.

"Time for some horrible coffee," said Clive.

"I know just the place," said Hector.

"Don't knock it," said Frank, as he looked for Ian's number and then pressed the button. "Some day they'll put a plaque on this building telling the world that it was here that members of the *cuadrilla* met and ceremonially drank Ian's horrible coffee before the *encierro*."

"That I doubt," said Clive.

229

"*Hermano,* you need to have more faith in the power of the *cuadrilla,*" said Hector, as the door opened. "We're a force to be reckoned with."

Upstairs in Ian's apartment Peter was looking at the paper to see which bulls were running, while Ian poured himself a cup of coffee.

"So, any intel on the bulls?" said Ian.

"Fuente Ymbro," said Peter.

"And what do we know about them?" Ian asked.

"Not much, but I got a pic of one of 'em, if you want to have a look," said Peter.

"OK, let's see," said Ian. He looked at the newspaper and the photograph of a jet-black bull, weighing in at approximately five hundred and seventy kilos. *Negro Amargo* they called it.

"Bitter Black," said Hector, "curious name for a bull."

"They couldn't just call him Pablo or Juan or Pepe? No, they had to come up with this fucked up name," said Ian.

"I kinda like it," said Frank, "reminds me of a cocktail straight out of Harlem in the 1930s. You know, smoke filled room, black tuxedoes, leggy dames."

"Oh for crying out loud, Ardito," said Ian, "we're talking about bulls, not jazz."

"Just sayin'," said Frank.

"And what's on the telly?" Ian asked Hector.

"It's a quarter to eight and they're about ready to let everyone out of the holding area."

"That's our cue, gentlemen, time to move," said Ian.

230

Outside they filtered into the crowd of runners, Peter walking back to the beginning of Mercaderes, while Ian chose a spot not too far from Bar Fitero. Hector also walked up Estafeta and Frank was with him. They stopped in front of Chez Belagua, the bar where the Irrinitzi *peña* members often met.

"This is where we'll hitch a ride with the bulls," said Hector.

"If all goes well," said Frank.

"No worries, my friend, we're going to have a kick-ass run today."

"If you say so."

"I say so and what's more I feel it," said Hector, "trust me on this one."

Frank looked at his watch, almost eight o'clock.

"*Suerte*," he said to Hector.

"*Tambien a ti, hermano*," Hector answered, and then they heard the first rocket, closely followed by the second.

The bulls were compact and moving fast up Santo Domingo where they knocked a runner out of their path before continuing to City Hall and the beginning of Mercaderes. Peter started his run on the corner of Chapitela and Mercaderes and stayed with the herd until just after the curve where he flattened himself against a wall to avoid getting tossed by one of the bulls.

Clive was running from the beginning of Estafeta and didn't see Peter's near miss. He was sprinting to catch up with the herd and tripped over another runner in front of him.

"They're coming," said Frank.

231

"See ya at Txoko!" said Hector, and before Frank could answer the herd had passed them and Hector had already sprinted to the right side of the road. He ran behind one of the steers until he saw an opening in the group and was able to position himself next to one of the bulls on the right. There were people running in front of the bulls, but not with them, and they were pushed out of the way or dived for safety wherever it was possible, as the herd rushed towards the Arena. At Telefónica Hector was ready to make his move for a run on the horns, but then the herd shifted to the right, as he entered the *callejón* and he was smashed against the tunnel wall. The bull that hit him was the last of the group and was separated from the rest of the herd. Seeing Hector on the ground it began to stake out its territory, goring Hector in his right and left thighs, in his abdomen and, finally, severing an aorta in his heart. A group of runners were eventually able to distract the bull and to carry Hector to an ambulance, but he died on the way to the hospital.

Chapter 27

There was no escaping it. The odds were against you in the long run. This is what Hector would have told him. He would have politely pointed out that everyone in their group knew the risks and that if one of them didn't survive then at least that person died doing what he loved most. Because that was the most important thing, Hector had always said, living your life to the fullest.

"What a load of crap," said Frank out loud. He was going down on record, to himself at least, that he did not agree with his friend. That even if the odds had been stacked against Hector it was still a fucking waste of a life, no matter how you looked at it. Why couldn't he have just climbed down from his manic high and ditched his feverish dreams of becoming a shaman into some deep, year long, clinical depression? That way he would still be here. But no, of course not, he had to go out in a flash of glory.

"Typical bipolar stunt. They never think of anyone but themselves," he cursed. He was angry and sad and there was nothing that he could do about it. Hector was gone and nothing was going to bring him back. What was done was done and now he had to break the bad news to Irina. He was walking back to the apartment from Txoko where he'd commiserated with the others. They were all in a state of shock and pretty much didn't know what to say, except that they loved the guy and that he'd be missed.

Before he left the *cuadrilla* they all agreed to meet up again that afternoon at the bullring for the *corrida*. Clive had said that it was important for them to be there to see the bull that had killed Hector die at the end of the matador's *faena*. He had insisted that Hector would have wanted it that way.

So, after spending the rest of the morning and most of the afternoon consoling Irina, the two of them met the others at the entrance to the bullring at a quarter to six. While Frank had his doubts about the importance of being there to see the bull die or that this might in some way satisfy Hector's ghost, there was one thing that he liked about the *corrida* that day. Before the first matador dedicated his performance to anyone or the first bull charged into the ring, before anything happened, there was a minute of silence for Hector with just the sound of a solo trumpet to lend the proper dignity and respect to their friend's passing.

When the music stopped there were cheers and applause from the spectators, both from the *peñas* and the seats in the *sombra* sections. What was important, thought Frank, was that neither the *corrida* nor the *fiesta* were cancelled and this was something very Spanish. It was as if they were reminding everyone that death was a part of being alive, that you could not have one without the other. In Spain they accepted this truth and lived their lives accordingly.

Chapter 28

The next morning Frank took a taxi to the airport south of Pamplona. He'd found out from the hospital that they were shipping Hector's body home that day and that the flight to Madrid left at 6:45 and that from there he'd go to New York, Los Angeles and finally San Diego where his parents would be waiting for him. Frank wanted to be there when he left, to pay his respects to Hector and to see him off on the last trip he would ever be taking anywhere.

He had told the others where he was going and not to wait up for him at Ian's. He didn't expect that anyone would join him and in fact none of them were there when the taxi dropped him off at the airport. Today was day nine of the *fiesta* and he knew that they would all do the *encierro* and run it where Hector had always run it, down at the *curva* on Estafeta. Of course, he understood why they were doing it, to honor his memory, and that was good for them, but not for Frank, not today.

He walked over to an information counter and explained to the two ladies, who were just getting things ready for the new day, why he was there and what he needed, and they called one of their colleagues from the shipping department, and after a few minutes a man showed up and took him to where he could see the coffin.

"*Era su amigo?* (Was he your friend?)" asked the employee, as they entered the baggage area.

"*Sí*," said Frank.

"*Mis condolencias* (my condolences)," said the baggage guy.

235

Frank was expecting to see a traditional heavy wooden casket, but instead it was something much more utilitarian, a metal casket inside a cardboard box. It had various adhesive straps that had been wrapped around the cardboard and was ticketed like the rest of the oversized luggage surrounding it.

"Take your time," said the man.

"*Gracias*," said Frank.

"I'll be over there if you need anything," he said, pointing to the desk where he normally worked.

Frank walked up to the coffin and knocked twice on the cardboard. "Hey Hector," he said. "Anyone home? I know you're in there, so if this is some kind of sick joke now's the time to spring out of your metal crate and watch me have a heart attack."

"Alright, I believe you," he continued, "but you have to admit this is weird. You've only been gone one day, and here I am talking to you while you're in a box. I mean, tell me that isn't strange shit. You, of all people, Mr. Manic himself, Mr. I look like a fucking god and fuck like one too, tell me that isn't totally screwed, *hermano*."

"No, don't tell me anything."

"There's no use in hiding it, brother. This hurts. I feel weak, like someone blew a hole right through me. It's a shitty situation, all around. But I just wanted you to know that I miss ya like hell and that you will always be for me my true brother, *mi hermano,* and that I will never forget you."

"Oh screw it, Hector, this is useless, I'm messing up your cardboard with these goddamn tears. Sorry about that," he apologized, as he wiped his eyes with the sleeve of his shirt.

"I gotta get out of here, brother, I'll talk to you later."

Chapter 29

For the rest of the *fiesta* they continued to go out and to party but it wasn't the same. The bacchanalia was winding down and on the last day neither Frank nor Irina went to the *corrida*. They did go to the *Pobre de mí*, the traditional closing ceremony of the *fiesta*. With Ian, Peter and Clive, they gathered with hundreds of others in front of the *Ayuntamiento,* holding candles and singing the words, "*Pobre de mí, pobre de mí, que se han acabado las fiestas de San Fermín,* (Poor me, poor me, the festival of San Fermin has ended). At midnight it was over, and everyone bid a sad "see you next year" to each other.

Early the next morning Frank and Irina took a train to Madrid where they stayed with friends. They were decompressing, said Frank, because after a *fiesta* like that you really needed a vacation. Neither of them spoke about Hector, and that was also part of their decompression. It would take time to truly accept what had happened to their friend. For Frank it was painful because Hector had been his brother, "his twin from another mother", as he liked to say, while for Irina it was even more complicated. She had been his lover and in her heart she had embraced him as her man, or at least the best of the many men that she had had during the *fiesta*.

What they both needed now was to move on, and Madrid was a city where they could do that. They started off with the museums, spending a day at the Prado and another at the Reina Sofia. They also went out to a number of restaurants and bars. In particular, Frank liked the rooftop bar at the Circulo de Bellas Artes for the view you could get of Madrid and of the Gran Via at sunset. Irina said that the view wasn't bad, but that she much preferred La Venencia, a sherry bar on Calle Echegaray, not too far from the Plaza del Sol. They spent an evening there, getting drunk on a bottle of Tio Pepe. The place had the look of a time capsule with tables, chairs and posters that seemed not to have changed since the nineteen fifties or forties. Even the ancient telephone on the wall with a mouthpiece and a receiver that you held close to your ear looked authentic. They didn't go to El Botín. Hemingway may have gone there after the *fiesta* but the idea of eating a suckling pig in the middle of July, in the oven like heat of Madrid, was something that Frank felt that they could do without. Instead, they took the advice of their friends and went to La Venta Del Oso, which was on the outskirts of the city and specialized in Austurian cuisine. Frank had a steak while Irina tried the monkfish, both of which were excellent.

Looking at the cognacs after dinner, Frank suggested they try the Courvoisier XO Imperíal. He also ordered an espresso, while Irina had tea. They continued to talk about the city and the places they had visited, including Los Arcos, the hacienda fifty kilometers northwest of Madrid, near the Escorial monastery, where their friend and host raised purebred Spanish horses for dressage and *rejoneo* (horseback bullfighting). They had spent an afternoon there, and Irina told Frank that the house and the fields and the horses were so beautiful and everything was so peaceful that she wouldn't mind coming back again. Frank didn't know what to tell her, in part because it was the sort of thing that anyone might say. His visits to Los Arcos and to Madrid to see his friends after the *fiesta* were something of a tradition, but he

239

wasn't at all sure if Irina could ever become a part of that tradition. Would they still be together in a year's time? Or rather, were they even together now? Frank knew that there were some women that had to wander, searching in vain through their younger years and as they grew older for god only knows what, a father figure, the perfect man, an adventure? Relationship did not come easy to them and they never stayed long. A year to three at the max and they were gone. Was Irina one of them, he asked himself? Who could say?

As she was drinking her tea, she asked Frank what his plans were.

"You mean for tomorrow?" said Frank, thinking that she had a flight back to Russia and that his to Los Angeles was the day after that.

"No, I mean for the future," said Irina, "for us."

"Is there an us?" he asked, half in jest and more than just a little surprised to hear her ask him about their "future".

"I think there is," she told him, "or, at least, there could be."

"We had a rough start," said Frank.

"We had a crazy start, but that was *fiesta*."

"*Fiesta* is the dream," he agreed, "but then you wake up."

"Perhaps it was just a beginning for the two of us? A kind of test to see if we would survive."

"Did we?"

"Survive?" she said. "I think we did, but we won't know for sure for some time, for years perhaps, and until that day…"

"…we could stay together," said Frank, finishing her thought and taking her hand, which was shaking, gently in his. In spite of

240

everything, he loved her and didn't want to let her go, and yet he couldn't say if her feelings were the same or if staying with him was just a way for her to postpone that moment when she would have to leave.

"We could live here," said Frank, casting his doubts aside. Life was about taking chances and he would take his with Irina, come what may.

"Yes," she said, almost in a whisper, with tears now running down her cheeks, "we could do that."

The End